THE
TRANSLUCENT
BOY
and the girl who
dreamed she could fly

by Tom Hoffman

Books by Tom Hoffman

*Paperback versions available online
at Amazon or Barnes & Noble*

Bartholomew the Adventurer • The Eleventh Ring
Bartholomew the Adventurer • The Thirteenth Monk
Bartholomew the Adventurer • The Seventh Medallion

•••

Orville Mouse and the Puzzle of the Clockwork Glowbirds
(audiobook available @ Audible)
Orville Mouse and the Puzzle of the Shattered Abacus
Orville Mouse and the Puzzle of the Capricious Shadows
Orville Mouse and the Puzzle of the Last Metaphonium
Orville Mouse and the Puzzle of the Sagacious Sapling

•••

The Translucent Boy and the Girl Who Saw Him
The Translucent Boy and the Cat Who Ran Out of Time
The Translucent Boy and the Girl Who Dreamed She Could Fly

•••

The Comet Kid Chronicles • Under the Blue Comet
The Comet Kid Chronicles • The Unfocused Man
The Comet Kid Chronicles • The Sinister Sorcerer

With lots of love for
Molly, Alex, Sophie, Oliver,
and Naomi

Table of Contents

For all the amazing
translucent kids out there
who spend their days
listening, reading,
and thinking.

"All journeys have secret destinations of which the traveler is unaware."

– Martin Buber

**"Not until we are lost
do we begin to
understand ourselves."**

– Henry David Thoreau

THE TRANSLUCENT BOY

and the girl who
dreamed she could fly

Chapter 1

You Don't Belong Here

Odo Whitley was pulled from his dream by the unexpected and perplexing sound of rushing, gurgling water. He yanked the pillow over his head, trying to block out the annoying noise, peering at his watch through half closed eyes. Who could be taking a bath at three o'clock in the morning? A whistling wind joined the sound of rushing water, this symphony of inexplicable sounds punctuated suddenly by a violent clap of thunder. Using a curious skill he had perfected as a translucent child, Odo pressed his hand against the wall, a twelve-inch circular section of it becoming transparent. He peered out into the night, his eyes on the streetlight in front of his house, expecting to see branches flailing wildly in the wind, rain spattering on the pavement, rivulets of water pouring off the roof. He saw none of these things; the night was still and clear and silent. A chill rolled through him when he realized the source of the sounds. He turned slowly, his eyes widening when he saw the torrent of water racing

3

across his bedroom floor.

The good news was it was a spectral river, a watery apparition, most likely one of his own creation. He climbed out of bed, stepping into his nocturnal vision, the wind rising to a dull roar, spray from ghostly whitecaps passing through his bedroom wall.

"This is like the ghost forest I saw before we went to Emerus. It's some kind of message, maybe a warning."

Odo was recalling his adventures on the world of Emerus, its dark primordial forests filled with huge sightless frogs and creepy orange slugs. Their search for his friend Silas' missing grandpa, the eccentric inventor who disappeared in 1921, had taken Odo, Sephie, and Silas to that distant world, where they successfully thwarted a deadly alien invasion, rescuing Mirus Ward and his two children, returning them safely to their world of 1921.

Odo eyed the rushing, churning water, now up to his waist. "Maybe we're going to visit a world filled with huge rivers. That would be kind of fun. I'll tell Sephie and Silas about this tomorrow, see what they say."

A week ago Sephie had told him that Doppel, the Emerusian robot who had fallen in love with her, had returned to his home planet after she told him Odo was her boyfriend. Doppel had given her a deeply romantic poem proclaiming his undying love for her, a poem Sephie had shown Odo, along with her best smirky smile.

"Isn't this a beautiful poem, Odo Whitley? Doppel wrote it just for me. You're not jealous, are you?"

"Why would I be jealous of a dumb robot? Besides, he didn't write it, he plagiarized it. It's called *How Do I Love Thee,* and was written by Elizabeth Barrett Browning in 1850."

Sephie raised her eyebrows. "You seem to know a lot about love poems, Odo Whitley."

Odo glared at her. "I read a lot of stuff, mostly science, and I remember it all. Did Doppel say if he's coming back?"

"He's not, he decided to help Kalumnia rebuild Emerus."

Odo grinned. "Great, sounds like fun. I'll miss him. He was nice, but kind of annoying."

"I liked it that he wasn't afraid to say how he felt about me." Sephie's smirk reappeared.

Odo's train of thought veered off the rails when he realized his clothes were soaking wet, icy cold water pressing against his skin, violent shivers running through him. He pushed his way over to the bed, climbing up onto it, the rising water pushing him against the wall. He was beginning to panic. This had never happened before; his ghostly vision had become alarmingly real. "I have to get out of here!"

He placed his hand on the bedroom wall, desperately trying to create a translucent exit from his flooded room. The good news was the shimmering doorway appeared, the bad news was his room abruptly vanished. He struggled wildly, fighting against the current, trying to keep his head above water. The sky was filled with dark roiling clouds, the wind howling and screaming, waves churning wildly, slapping violently against him.

"Odo Whitley! Odo! Come back!"

"Odo!"

Odo twisted around, his eyes on a shadowy shoreline, three figures waving at him. "It's Sephie and Silas and someone I don't know!" He raised one arm, trying to wave, but slipped beneath the surface, then bobbed back up again, gasping for air. "Help!"

The roar of the wind and the pounding torrents of rain drowned out his cries and the cries of his friends.

Panic set in. He was getting tired and the water was freezing cold. Could he drown here? Freeze to death? Was this place real? Water sloshed into his mouth, up his nose. He choked, thrashing wildly in the frothing water. This was more than real, he could die here.

The moment he realized he had to get to shore or he would drown was the moment something slammed into him, his head banging painfully against a hard surface. He let out a cry, certain some horrific aquatic monstrosity was about to devour him. He whipped around, giving a cry when he saw the thirty-foot long boat next to him, the rustic wooden craft rocking wildly in the raging water.

"Help me!" He clawed at the side of the boat, trying to pull himself up, stopping when he saw a scruffy old bearded man in a coarsely woven brown robe staring down at him with cold black eyes.

"What are you doing here?"

"I'm drowning!" Odo could feel his grip on the boat

slipping. He also noticed he wasn't translucent, which meant two things; this was a real world, and it wasn't Earth. "A little help?"

"You don't belong here!"

"Really? I don't belong here? Really?"

The old man scowled, hitting Odo's hand with a heavy wooden paddle. He let out a yelp of pain, slipping back into the frigid waters. "What are you doing? I'll drown!"

"You don't belong here! There's no free lunches, boy!"

The disheveled old man pushed Odo beneath the surface with his long paddle, Odo struggling wildly. He was going to drown. This was the end, he was going to drown on some stupid alien planet in a stupid river that he never wanted to–"

The raging water faded to nothingness, Odo finding himself floating in a warm, infinitely vast darkness. "Whoa. What is this? Am I dead? Did I drown? I don't feel the water anymore. Maybe this is what happens when you…"

He froze when the gentle voice sounded in his thoughts. *"A gift of great joy and great sorrow; what was lost shall be found."*

"Who are you? What does that mean?"

Odo waited in the dark void for an answer, but none came. He was exhausted from his struggles in the river, barely able to keep his eyes open. "So tired. I hope I'm not dead. That would be bad."

Odo Whitley awoke to the sound of someone knocking on his bedroom door, a familiar voice calling out to him.

"Odo, rise and shine! You don't want to be late for school. Breakfast is ready."

"Okay, I'm getting up, Mom." Odo groaned. The good news was he wasn't dead, the bad news was he had no idea where he'd been, who the crazy old homicidal boat guy was, and why Sephie and Silas were in his vision.

Chapter 2

Emmeline Snow

Emmeline Snow leaned back in her grandma's wooden rocking chair, her eyes on the smooth silver walls surrounding her. She was safe in the Cube; no one could hurt her, no one could laugh at her, no one could pity her. Her legs were straight and strong here. She felt powerful, in control. The Cube was Emmeline's safe place, a haven she had created with her mind. For almost a year she had visualized the Cube as she drifted off to sleep, imagining its smooth impregnable gleaming walls, a feeling of warmth and security filling her.

She remembered the night she woke up inside her dream, inside the fully formed Cube, a world which had suddenly become more real to her than the one she was born in.

The Cube was empty except for the rocking chair and a blinking keypad next to the door. It had taken over a month to find the passcode to open the door, a five digit code someone had scratched into the ceiling. She was certain it had been Nomi, the gentle being she heard but never saw, her benevolent invisible guide in the world of dreams.

She stood up, striding over to the door, tapping in the five digit passcode. As the door whirred open she wondered what manner of world would be waiting for her. They were always different, some scary and wild and violent, some peaceful, stunningly beautiful. She knew she was safe here, even in the scary worlds. Nothing could hurt her.

The door slid open, the pungent aroma of salt air wafting into the Cube, the rhythmic sound of distant waves crashing onto the shore. She eyed the dense jungle foliage, a striped green snake slithering up one of the gnarled vines, its black tongue flicking in and out.

She stepped out onto the spongy forest floor, curious humming sounds coming from above. Looking up, she spotted a group of large flying insects swooping and soaring above the forest canopy, their long colorful tails flowing behind them. There were two suns in the sky, one of them red.

She followed a well traveled forest path, heading toward the sound of the waves, soon arriving at a pristine white sandy beach, the glorious scent of sea air filling her nostrils, blue green waves rolling like clockwork onto the shore, leaving behind sparkling white bubbles of foam.

"This is nice. I like this world. It's wild and natural and beautiful." She frowned when she spotted a gleaming city in the distance. "People." Maybe they were an advanced race; gentle, understanding, kind. Or they could be aggressive and violent, a race of brutal conquerors and invaders. It didn't matter either way, nothing could hurt her here.

She turned when she heard the rustling noise behind her, a six-legged red and yellow hard shelled creature stepping out of the jungle, unfazed by Emmeline's presence. It crept along the beach to a tangle of dripping wet seaweed, munching on it with razor sharp mandibles.

"Hey, dream creature, can you talk?"

The creature did not respond.

"Enjoy your lunch, buddy." Emmeline waved to it, heading down the beach, hoping to get a better view of the city. That was when she heard the scream. Someone or something needed help.

Racing across the sand into the jungle, she pushed her way through the thick green foliage, emerging into a large grassy clearing. The source of the terrified scream was a short, vaguely human creature with blue wrinkly skin, two arms, two legs, a head, and large pale green round eyes. It was dressed in a sparkling green tunic, shiny black boots, some form of electronic device strapped to its belt. This was not a primitive being. The creature stood facing a ferocious looking furry white beast raised up on its hind legs, its long jet black ears pressed back against its head, the universal sign of aggression. Emmeline studied its six-inch long blood red claws. This was definitely a dangerous predator. The blue creature was shaking violently, unable to run. It was either paralyzed with fear, or the white beast was

11

manipulating its neural pathways. She'd seen that in other worlds.

Emmeline stepped forward, hollering at the creature. "Hey, furball! You want some of this?"

The beast turned slowly, studying her, inching toward her, emitting a low vicious growl. It opened its mouth, revealing a long black tongue and two rows of needle sharp teeth.

Six months ago Emmeline would have screamed and woken up, but that was before she visited a world she called Land of the Lizards. She had been walking across a broiling hot desert when six scaly lizard people armed with short wooden bows popped up out of the sand. One of them fired an arrow at her, barely missing. Another one fired, Emmeline swatting the arrow out of the air. "Nice try, dream lizard."

The lizard hissed, shooting another arrow, Emmeline knocking it aside before it hit her. That was the first time Nomi spoke to her.

"Don't block the arrows, let them pass through you. Nothing can hurt you here. You are safe."

"Who are you?" She swatted another arrow aside.

"I am Nomi, your guide."

"What kind of guide?"

"Let the arrows pass through you. They will not harm you."

Emmeline sighed. Nomi was probably right, she couldn't get hurt in a dream. She lowered her arms, her eyes on the lizard creatures. Three of them raised their bows and fired, the arrows passing harmlessly through her. The lizards jumped up and down, making shrill chirping noises, then fired again, the arrows passing through her again. When she walked toward them they ran off, disappearing behind a dune. She grinned. "Thanks, Nomi."

The towering white furry beast was now only a dozen feet from Emmeline, putrid green slime dripping from its mouth.

"Whew! When's the last time you brushed your teeth, buddy?"

The creature's unblinking red eyes were on Emmeline. There was a sudden blur of motion, the beast leaping forward, letting out a howl of pain when it passed through her, smashing into a spiky gnarled tree trunk. It turned in surprise, staring at her, rubbing its arm.

"That's so embarrassing, crashing into a tree like that. I'll tell you what, it can be our little secret. I won't tell your friends how silly you looked."

The beast turned with a low growl, disappearing into the forest. She heard a voice in her head, but it wasn't Nomi.

"You saved my life."

She turned to the blue creature with the round green eyes.

"What are you doing out here?"

"I was exploring the park. I wanted to study the creatures who live here."

"Where do you live?"

"In the city. I didn't tell my parents where I was

13

going."

"How old are you?"

"I'm still a pod. My name is Eloy."

"I'm guessing that means you're a kid. I'll take you home. Have you ever flown before?"

"My parents have two floaters. They go really fast."

"I'm talking about flying without a ship."

"That's impossible."

Emmeline grinned. "Take my hand, Eloy."

Eloy took Emmeline's outstretched hand, giving a yelp when they floated up above the jungle, soaring across the sky toward the sparkling glass city.

Chapter 3

Silas Ward

Emmeline Snow rolled over in bed when her alarm went off. It was her first day at the new school, the first day of kids gawking at her. They wouldn't know about her brother, but they would know about her legs. She climbed out of bed, grabbing her cane. No way was she taking it to school. Pulling on her clothes, she headed down the stairs, gripping the handrail tightly. She had breakfast, then made her lunch, slipping it into her backpack.

"Mom! I'm leaving!"

There was no answer. She sighed, heading back up the stairs, tapping on her mom's bedroom door.

"Mom?"

Still no answer.

She cracked the door open. "Mom, I'm leaving for school."

"What time is it?"

"The bus will be here in five minutes."

"I'm sorry, sweetie, I had a late night showing houses. I think I may have sold one. Do you want me to make you lunch?"

"I already made it. I have to go or I'll miss the bus."

"Okay. Have a good first day at school. Try to make some friends. Love you."

"I will. Love you too." Emmeline looked down at her twisted legs. She knew she wouldn't be making any friends. "Bye."

Ten minutes later, after she had declined the bus driver's offer to help her onto the bus, Emmeline hobbled down the aisle, taking a seat by herself, looking out the window, ignoring the stares of the other kids, trying to imagine herself safely in the Cube.

Two stops later a boy strolled down the aisle, plopping down on the seat next to her. She held her backpack in front of her like a suit of armor, avoiding eye contact with him.

"Hi, I'm Silas Ward. You must be new."

Emmeline gave him a quick nod and looked away, gazing out the window.

Silas eyed her curiously, his eyes widening slightly when he saw the ghost standing next to her. Interesting. It was a boy about their age, his eyes on Emmeline. Silas sent him a thought.

"Do you know her?"

The ghost didn't reply. Silas shrugged. Sometimes they talked and sometimes they didn't. He looked at Emmeline, noting how she was hugging her backpack close to her. It was familiar to him; he'd done the same thing for years, back when he was terrified of ghosts, back when he was being bullied by Brandon Crouch, before he met Odo and Sephie, before they taught him that seeing ghosts was a gift, not a curse. He grinned to himself, remembering their adventures on Emerus, how the ghost of Odo's grandpa had helped them out of some very precarious predicaments.

"How long have you lived in Bedford Falls?"

Emmeline turned slightly, still avoiding eye contact. "I just moved here with my mom."

"You'll like it here. It's a good school and the kids are nice. It won't take you long to make friends."

She nodded slightly, wondering if he had noticed her legs.

Five minutes later the bus shuddered to a stop in the school parking lot, the door squealing open, kids pouring out, running and hollering toward the front door.

Silas watched Emmeline get to her feet. "I can carry your backpack if you want. Do you know where your homeroom is?"

"I don't need any help." Emmeline headed down the aisle, Silas studying her awkward gait, noting how her left foot was twisted inward, her right leg crooked. He also noted the ghost boy was walking next to her. There was a sad story here somewhere, but he didn't know what it was. This was a girl with a lot of secrets. She was also kind of cute.

Silas hopped off the bus, heading to the main entrance, making his way down the hall to his locker.

17

"Silas!"

He spun around at the sound of Sephie Crumb's voice, waving to her, focusing on the translucent figure next to her. "Hey, Sephie! Hey, Odo!" He ran over to them, Sephie grabbing his arm.

"Is it true?"

"Is what true?"

"You broke up with Nia?"

Silas nodded. "It's true. We're history."

Odo said, "I thought you guys were best friends?"

"I thought so too until I told her I could see ghosts."

"You told her? What did she say?"

"She said she couldn't be around someone like that. She seemed scared of ghosts and probably scared of me."

Sephie gave him a comforting smile, her eyes studying his head. "Ghosts can be really scary to some people. Are you doing okay?"

"Are you reading my brainwaves, Encephalo Girl?"

Sephie laughed. "Maybe a little, just checking to see how you're doing. Breaking up with someone is not easy."

"I'm fine. I guess I was kind of expecting it. I was terrified of ghosts before I met you guys. I knew I was taking a chance telling her, but I didn't want to keep any secrets from her, especially a big one like that."

Odo nodded. "I remember how scared I was when we followed the Lady in Black down into your basement."

"If it wasn't for you guys I never would have figured

out she was my grandma."

"Us superheroes have to stick together, Ghostwatch-er."

Sephie rolled her eyes, then said. "Silas, did I tell you about the poem Doppel gave me?"

Odo glared at her. "Enough about that ridiculous love poem."

"Odo said Doppel went back to Emerus?"

Odo nodded. "He did indeed. No more crazy robots plagiarizing mushy old love poems."

Silas knew exactly why Odo was glad Doppel was gone. "We should go see Wikerus Praevian, see how he and Mrs. Preke are doing."

Sephie nodded. "Maybe he'll have a cool adventure for us."

Silas said, "I forgot to tell you, Mrs. Preke hired me to work for the Serendipity Salvage Company."

"Nice. Welcome aboard, newbie." Odo slapped him on the back

Sephie looked at him, her eyes narrowing.

"Why are you looking at me like that?"

"You're hiding something. Something scary."

"No, I'm not."

"Spill it, Odo Whitley."

"Fine. I had a really weird vision last night. There was a river running through my room and I almost drowned after this crazy guy in a wooden boat pushed me under the water. You guys were both there, standing on the shore. There was someone else with you, a girl, but I didn't recognize her."

"How could you almost drown in a vision?"

"That was the weird part, it started out as a vision, then turned real."

"You went to a real world?"

"I think so, but I'm not sure."

"We can ask Wikerus about it."

Silas said, "You have no idea who the strange girl was?"

"She was in the shadows, I couldn't see her face."

"Did you notice anything different about her legs?"

"What do you mean?"

"Nothing, just curious."

Sephie studied Silas, an imperceptible smile crossing her face.

Chapter 4

The Pen

The next day was Saturday, Odo getting up bright and early. He and Sephie and Silas were going to the movies that afternoon, but he had decided to spend the morning working.

When Mrs. Preke had hired him to work for the Serendipity Salvage Company, she gave him an envelope containing five hundred dollars and what she called his work ring. When he wanted to work, he should put the ring on, and when he was done working, he should take the ring off.

It had taken him some time to understand exactly what the work ring did. When he wore it, a series of odd coincidences would occur, as if the ring was guiding him toward some unseen destination. The first time he wore it, the ring had guided him to Sephie Crumb's house, then taken them both to Wikerus Praevian's house, the Fortisian who taught them about interdimensional shifting using waystones. Odo's job was to follow the path of the ring, although sometimes it was hard to know which events were being caused by the ring and which were not.

"Okay, here we go." He opened his dresser drawer and pulled out the silver ring, reading the Latin inscription on the inner surface.

aperi oculos tuos et vide

It was Sephie who had translated the inscription for him – open your eyes and see. He slipped the ring on and headed downstairs. Odo was aware that his parents still had a difficult time noticing him when he entered a room. Several times he had been sitting at the table when they began to argue or talk about him, not realizing he was there. To prevent embarrassing incidents such as those from happening, he usually made a monumentally bombastic entrance.

"Odo Whitley is in the house! All hail Odo!"

"Good heavens, Odo, you don't have to holler that out every time you come into the kitchen. I heard you coming down the stairs."

"Sorry, Mom. Where's Dad?"

"He had to work today. They're introducing a new line of Chocko CrunchCakes called Golden CrunchCake Delights. It was your dad's idea, so he's in charge of it."

"Nice. I hope he doesn't expect me to eat any of them."

"Your dad works hard. It's not the career he wanted,

but he's making the best of it."

"I'm sorry, I know he works hard. They're just... you know... so crunchy."

"You need to walk Mrs. Beasley's dog for me today."

"Why can't you do it?"

"I'm busy, I have to go somewhere. Something came up."

Odo looked at her curiously. "Where do you have to go?"

"I'm going to visit a new store called *None of Odo's Business*."

Odo burst out laughing. "Good one! I'll have to remember that and use it on Sephie."

Petunia grinned. "I didn't think it up by myself, I saw it on a TV show."

"It's still funny."

"So you'll walk Tiny?"

"Their dog is named Tiny? Let me guess, he's as big as a horse?"

"Yes, isn't it funny that they named him Tiny when he's so big?"

"Hilarious. They should have called him Neutrino."

Odo's mom looked slightly annoyed. "I don't know what that means, Odo. Is it a joke?"

"A neutrino is a subatomic particle similar to an electron, but has no electrical charge so it–"

"I have to go or I'll be late. The key is under the doormat, Tiny's leash is hanging next to the front door."

"Okay, have fun wherever you're going."

Petunia grinned. "See you later."

Odo finished breakfast, rinsed the dishes, and headed out the front door. The very last thing he wanted to do was walk some ridiculously big dog. He stopped short, remembering he was wearing his work ring. Maybe that's why he was walking Tiny. This was an unusual event, the first time his mom had ever asked him to walk the dog. He raised one eyebrow. "The game is afoot, Watson."

Ten minutes later Odo reached under the Beasley's welcome mat, retrieving a brass door key. He inserted it in the lock, jumping back when the ferocious barking sounded, something heavy thudding against the front door, rattling the windows. Odo groaned. "This thing is going to kill me."

He cracked the door open, bracing himself, inching inside. Before he had time to react, the huge mastiff leaped on him, licking his face, gobs of slimy drool running down his cheeks.

"That's disgusting! It's on my lips! Get off me, you crazy giant dog!" He pushed it away, eyeing the enormous beast as it stood panting in front of him. "You're almost as tall as I am. Wait, you can see me?" The dog tilted his head. "Nice, I guess dogs can see translucent people." Odo grabbed the leash from the hook, Tiny barking and jumping toward him. "Yes, we're going for a walk, just me and the Hound of the Baskervilles. Maybe we'll get lucky and find someone you can have for breakfast."

He snapped the leash onto Tiny's collar and they

headed out the front door. Much to Odo's surprise, Tiny was very well behaved, obediently strolling along next to him, sniffing the ground, not tugging on the leash.

"This isn't so bad. Mrs. Beasley did a good job of training him. Now I just have to keep my eyes open for strange coincidental events. Maybe I'm supposed to meet someone. It could be someone who knows something about my crazy old boat guy vision, maybe a formshifting alien."

Tiny gave a low growl.

"Just kidding about the alien." He patted Tiny's head.

As they headed down the sidewalk Odo noticed a man striding rapidly toward them. "This could be the guy."

The man approached, stepping to one side as he passed, his wary eyes on Tiny, not even noticing translucent Odo.

"Guess it wasn't him. Whoever it is will probably be able to see me."

A few minutes later Odo spotted an old man with a long white beard sitting on the front steps of a somewhat decrepit old house. "Bingo, this has to be the guy. Tiny, check out his beard. His coat looks a little like a cloak, he might be a wizard. Probably has cool powers like Sephie does."

Tiny looked at Odo, tilting his head. As they drew closer to the house, Odo formulated his plan. He would casually wave to the man, saying something like "Nice day, isn't it?" That would break the ice, giving the wizard a chance to introduce himself, maybe use some of his cool powers.

Odo was about to call out his cordial greeting when something profoundly unexpected happened. A big black cat with white feet leaped over the picket fence, streaking down the sidewalk. Tiny yanked the leash from Odo's hand, racing after the cat, his ferocious barking echoing through the neighborhood.

Odo chased after him, hollering, "Tiny! Tiny! Come back here!"

He saw the cat run into someone's yard, Tiny only a few feet behind. When Odo arrived, the cat was sitting on a branch ten feet up in the air licking its paw, gazing down at Tiny.

"Come here, you!" Odo grabbed Tiny's leash, wrapping it tightly around his wrist. "Don't even think about trying that again, you crazy dog. No more chasing cats. We have to go back and meet that old wizard."

Tiny growled as they headed out of the yard. "Knock it off. No growling." Odo gave a backwards glance at the cat, yelping when he saw it jump to the ground, racing through the yard toward them.

"What is wrong with that crazy cat?" He grabbed the leash with both hands, holding it tight as the cat raced past, hissing loudly at Tiny.

Odo never had a chance, tumbling to the ground when Tiny leaped forward, dragging him across the grass, stopping only when Odo's body got stuck between two thorny rose bushes.

"Ow! I'm going to clobber you, you crazy dog!

Unhh, something is stabbing me!" Odo rolled over, grabbing his leg, his eyes on the half buried object jabbing his leg.

"What is that thing?" Odo pulled it out of the ground, examining it. "A pen. Great, I got stabbed by a stupid pen. I'll probably need five tetanus shots." He wiped the dirt off the pen. "It's a nice one. Fancy. Engraved gold, looks like 18 carat. It could be worth a lot." He blinked when he saw the tiny flashing violet light on top of the pen. "Why would a pen have a light on it?"

Odo jumped to his feet, staring at the pen. "This is it! This is what the work ring wanted me to find, not that old guy with the white beard. This is no ordinary pen. Let's go, Tiny, I have to show this to Sephie and Silas. We need to figure out what it does and where it came from."

Chapter 5

Clawface

Later that afternoon, Odo, Sephie, and Silas were heading down Expergo Street toward the Excelsior II movie theatre. Odo and Silas were laughing, Sephie was not.

"There is something wrong with your brain, Odo Whitley. I can't believe you picked *Clawface* for our movie. I should get to pick the next two movies to make up for this travesty."

"There's nothing wrong with my brain, and it's not a travesty. It sounds like an amazing movie with a lot of depth to it, probably very educational. A terrifying creature named Clawface escapes from Hades and comes to Earth through a burbling tar pit. There's probably a lot of fascinating references to mythological creatures."

Sephie snorted. "Right. What does Clawface do when he gets to Earth, teach Greek philosophy at Harvard?"

Silas laughed. "He does Clawface stuff. In the pre-views it shows him creeping up on a girl having a picnic."

Sephie frowned. "It sounds awful. I get to pick the next two movies. I'm keeping my eyes closed for the whole show. It also sounds like nonsense, a creature named Clawface escaping from Hades? I'm going to need two bags of popcorn and a box of candy to get through this, Odo Whitley."

"Fine, I have lots of money. I just got my check from Serendipity Salvage. I'm rollin' in the dough."

Silas laughed. "This is going to be so fun. It sounds really good."

Sephie eyed Silas. "I know you and Nia just broke up, but is there another girl you like?"

"Why would you ask that?"

Sephie studied his brainwaves, a grin appearing on her face. "No reason."

"Why are you grinning? Are you reading my brain-waves?"

"Of course not, I was just thinking of something funny Odo said."

"Odo said something funny? Is that even a thing?"

Odo looked suitably offended. "What's that sup-posed to mean? I say lots of funny stuff. Everybody knows that."

Twenty minutes later the three friends were seated in the theatre, Sephie peering between her fingers at the flickering screen.

"This doesn't make sense. Why is she having a

picnic all by herself next to a big stinky burbling tar pit?"

Odo shrugged. "It's just part of the plot. Maybe she's a paleontologist taking a break from fossil hunting."

Silas laughed. "She might be a paleontologist now, but pretty soon she's going to be toast."

Odo slapped his leg. "Good one!"

"What's Clawface doing?"

"I think he's picking a flower."

"Why isn't he clobbering her?"

Sephie lowered her hand, her eyes on the screen. "He's giving her the flower."

"What is this? Why is he doing that?"

Sephie said, "Shhh, I'm trying to watch. I think he likes her. It's kind of sweet."

Odo let out a groan. "I want a refund."

"Too late, Odo Whitley."

"Give me that popcorn, and half your candy."

A long silence followed, broken by Silas' exasperated groan. "They're having dinner in a fancy restaurant and no one is even looking at Clawface? His face is covered with claws, how could they not notice that? Do you think for one second if my face was covered with claws people wouldn't notice me if I sat down in a restaurant?"

Sephie said, "Quiet. Most aliens look different than us, but most of them are really nice. Except for the ones who try to kill us. It's not how you look, it's what kind of person you are."

"I know that, I'm just saying the trailer was intentionally extremely misleading. They never once mentioned anything about romance."

"It's a romantic comedy. Haven't you been listening? Clawface is really funny. He's so cute. I don't think the claws on his face bother her at all, because he's so nice to her."

"I feel sick. Is it over yet?"

"I bet they get married."

Odo groaned. "I can't watch this." He whispered to Silas, "Check out this cool pen I found. It has a little purple light on it." He handed the gold pen to Silas.

"Nice. It's monogrammed. Hard to read, but I think it says GMB. It must be the owner's initials."

"What do you think the light is for?"

"I don't know, maybe for writing in the dark?"

"It's not bright enough, and it's on top of the pen."

"True. Does it work?"

"I haven't tried it yet." Odo pulled a piece of paper from his coat pocket, clicking the pen.

"The light turned yellow. Try writing your name."

Odo said, "That's weird, I can't write it. It wrote something else."

"What do you mean?"

"It wrote three numbers, 110."

"Try it again."

"110 again. I try to write my name but it just writes 110."

"Try to write my name."

"110."

"Give it to me, I want to try."

Sephie grabbed Odo's arm. "Shhhh! People are trying to watch the movie. Put that away. No talking."

Odo glared at her, slipping the pen into his pocket.

Silas glanced behind them, whispering, "Don't look now, but there are three ghosts watching the movie."

"Really? Ghosts watch movies?"

"These ones do. One of them is laughing. You know how much ghosts like romantic comedies." He snorted.

"It would be kind of cool being a ghost. I could get into the movies for free. And into ball games. Do you know how much it costs to go to a baseball game now? It's ridiculous. Who can afford that? Do you think ghosts would get scared watching a movie about ghosts?"

"It depends. If the ghosts watching the movie were nice, but the ghosts in the movie were creepy, they'd probably get scared. It's like asking if people would be scared watching a movie about people."

"It's not at all like that. Ghosts are innately scary by their very nature."

"No they're not, they're not scary at all. They're just people without bodies."

"Seriously? They moan and make creaky noises in the night. What's not scary about that?"

"That's just in the movies."

"You should go talk to the ghosts, see if they like the show. Ask them if Clawface is scary, or if they think he's funny."

"I'm not going to disturb them, Odo. The last thing I want is three angry ghosts yelling at me." Silas failed to mention that the ghost sitting two rows behind them was the boy who had been standing next to Emmeline. He was also looking directly at Silas.

Odo glanced up at the screen. "Really? They're kissing? The girl is kissing Clawface? Eww. Worst movie ever."

As the final credits rolled, Sephie leaned back in her seat. "That was such a good movie, Odo Whitley. So romantic. I don't need to pick the next two, we can just take turns like we always do."

"So we're going to see two romantic movies in a row? You should have to pick a scary movie next time to make up for this one."

"Nice try, Odo Whitley. You should have done more research before you picked it. It's called doing your due diligence."

Odo pulled the gold pen from his pocket, handing it to Sephie. "See my cool new pen? Try it, it works really well."

Silas grinned.

Sephie studied Odo's face. "I don't need to read your brainwaves to know you're up to something. Will it squirt water at me? Explode? Is it a talking pen that will say, 'Odo Whitley needs a new brain?'"

"It's not a trick, I promise, but it's not an ordinary pen. I found it when I was wearing my work ring."

"That's different. Give it to me."

Odo handed her the pen and paper. "Try writing your name."

Sephie shook her head. "I can't do it; it won't write

it. It only writes 420."

"Not 110?"

"Just 420."

"This is so weird. I can only write 110."

"Let me try it." Silas reached over and took the pen.

"Can you write your name?"

"No, but it's writing a word, not a number."

"What's the word?"

"Tectus."

"What does that mean?"

"I have no idea."

Sephie said, "It's Latin, it means a secret, or something hidden."

"Spooky."

Silas said, "Can I borrow it? There's something I want to try."

"What are you going to try?"

"I can't tell you. It's a big tectus."

Sephie laughed. "I see what you did there, Silas." She was also pretty sure she knew exactly what Silas was going to do with the pen.

Chapter 6

I See Ghosts

Silas waved to a friend as he boarded the school bus, strolling down the aisle. He spotted Emmeline and decided to be brave, to take the seat next to her. She glanced at him, quickly turning away.

He did his best to sound casual, cool. "How's it going?"

Emmeline didn't look at him. "Okay."

"Have a good weekend? Do anything fun?" His grandpa had told him if you treat someone like an old friend, they'll act like an old friend.

She turned, making brief eye contact. "I helped my mom do some stuff."

Silas nodded. "Cool. I'm Silas, in case you forgot. What's your name?"

"Emmeline."

"Nice. I went to the movies with my friends Odo and Sephie this weekend. We saw Clawface." Silas suddenly felt sick. How stupid was that? Why had he said that? She was going to think he was a lunatic who liked bloody horror movies. "Um, it's not what it sounds like. It wasn't scary, no stabbing or anything. He... uh... Clawface gave the tar pit girl a flower and... they went to dinner and no one noticed that he had claws on his face, which was kind of weird." He realized he was rambling. Why was he rambling? This was bad. He was in too deep now, more words would just make it worse. She'd never talk to him again. His face turned a remarkable shade of red.

"Sounds fun." Emmeline looked away. Silas' red face confirmed what she already knew. He didn't really want to be there. He was trying to be nice to the disabled girl with the twisted legs, but it made him painfully uncomfortable to be around her. He was probably embarrassed for her.

Silas groaned. He was an idiot. Why had he mentioned that stupid movie? He grabbed his pack when the bus rattled to a stop, standing up, nodding to Emmeline. "See you."

She nodded, but didn't say anything. Silas headed down the aisle. "Well done, maniac, now she thinks you're a total psycho lunatic."

Three classes later the lunch bell sounded, Silas having partially recovered from his disastrous encounter on the bus with Emmeline. His heart sank when he spotted the ghost boy at the classroom door, motioning for Silas to follow him. This was not good. He sent out a thought. *"What do you want?"*

The ghost boy pointed to the open door.

Silas groaned, getting to his feet. He didn't want to follow the ghost, but he felt as though he should, like he was being pulled by some unknown force. He grabbed his pack and headed out the door, following Ghost Boy down the hall. "Maybe I am a psycho lunatic."

Three minutes later he was in the cafeteria, the ghost pointing to Emmeline. She was sitting alone eating her lunch.

"No way, Ghost Boy. She already thinks I'm a lunatic. If I go over there now she'll think I'm a homicidal stalker."

The ghost held out his hand, Silas cringing when he saw the black metal spike he was holding. *"What is that? Did you murder someone with that? Are you a murder ghost?"*

The ghost pointed to himself, then pointed to Emmeline, motioning for Silas to go to her.

"You want to murder her with the spike? Are you insane?"

Ghost Boy shook his head.

"Who did you murder? What do you want me to do?"

The ghost pointed to Silas' eyes, then to himself, then to Emmeline.

"Wait, you want me to tell her I see you?"

The ghost nodded.

"No way, pal. Not ever. Not going to happen. A lunatic homicidal stalker tells a girl who's sitting alone that he can see a ghost who probably murdered someone with a big metal spike? Not a chance, Ghost

Boy."

The ghost boy put his hands together, clearly pleading with Silas.

Silas stared at him, his face softening. *"You don't need to beg. She already thinks I'm crazy. Fine, I guess it can't get any worse than it already is. I'm so doomed."*

He walked slowly over to Emmeline's table, taking a seat across from her. She looked up at him.

"Why do you keep sitting next to me?"

Silas took a deep breath. "I don't exactly know why."

She studied his face curiously. "What does that mean?"

"You're going to think I'm totally insane, but I need to tell you a secret."

"I don't like secrets. You should leave."

"Wait, it's important. I can't tell you why, but I'm supposed to tell you I see ghosts."

Emmeline blinked, her face turning to stone. "I get it, let's prank the crippled girl? Tell her you see ghosts? Then laugh about it with your friends?"

"It's not that, I promise. Ask my friends Odo and Sephie, they'll tell you it's true. I really do see ghosts."

"You need to seriously stay away from me. Leave me alone." Emmeline stood up, grabbing her backpack. She turned, heading for the door.

Silas slumped down in his chair. "That went well. She'll probably call the police and I'll get fifty years in prison."

Ghost Boy was staring at him, the metal spike still clutched in his hand. Silas glared at him. *"Happy now? Why don't you leave me alone and go murder someone with your stabby spike."*

Emmeline Snow was halfway across the cafeteria when she stopped, glancing back at Silas. He was eating his lunch and he did not look happy. She realized his face was not the face of a person who would try to prank a disabled girl. He looked almost sad. Maybe she'd misjudged him, maybe he was different, like her, didn't fit in. Maybe this world wasn't real to him. Maybe he lived in a world of ghosts. A shiver rolled through her. Maybe he could talk to her brother.

She turned around, crossing the cafeteria, sitting across from him, his eyes wide at the sight of her.

"Tell me about the ghosts."

"You don't think I'm insane?"

"Are you?"

The words tumbled out of his mouth. "No, I'm really not. I've seen ghosts my whole life. So did my Grandpa. I was so scared of them when I was little. There was this ghost in my house I called the Lady in Black. She used to walk down the stairs almost every night and go down into the basement. I'd pull a blanket over my head so she wouldn't see me. I was terrified of her."

Silas watched Emmeline's face change, the suspicion and fear transforming to a look of empathy.

"Did you ever find out who she was?"

"I did, thanks to my friends Odo and Sephie. They know a lot of stuff that most people don't. They told me not to be scared, told me what ghosts were, that the Lady in Black wasn't actually walking down the stairs every night, that she had only done it once, but the event had echoed across time."

"What happened?"

"We followed her down into the basement and watched her bury a little box. It's a really long story, but it turns out she was my Grandma, not scary at all. The story was sad, but it had a happy ending."

"Do you see ghosts in school?"

"I see them everywhere. I'm so used to it now I don't even think about it. They're just like normal people walking around but they're ghosts, people without physical bodies."

"So it's true that people don't really die?" Emmeline's eyes were sharp, focused.

"Their physical body does, but their true self, their consciousness doesn't. They're still the same person, just without a body. The ghosts I see in school are mostly people in old fashioned clothes walking next to kids. They're usually grandparents who stayed behind to watch over their grandkids."

"That makes me want to cry."

Silas blinked. That was a completely unexpected reaction. "It's okay, the ghosts aren't sad at all, they just want to help. Dying isn't sad to them because they see the world differently than we do, they know lots of stuff that we don't know."

"What kind of stuff?"

"That the universe is way bigger and way more

complicated than most people think it is. That there are lots of other worlds and dimensions filled with living beings that we don't know about."

Emmeline stared at Silas. "I can't believe you're saying all this."

"Does it sound crazy? Do you think I'm a lunatic?"

"No, I think I just made my first friend here."

Silas couldn't believe his luck, couldn't stop grinning. He decided not to tell her about Ghost Boy just yet; he didn't want to mess things up. "I should introduce you to my friends Odo and Sephie. They're really nice and they would totally like you."

It was the first time he'd seen Emmeline smile.

"That sounds fun." She decided not to ask him about her brother just yet; she didn't want to mess things up.

Chapter 7

A Secret Revealed

Odo and Sephie darted up to Silas as he was opening his locker. "Who's that girl you were sitting with at lunch?"

"What girl?"

Sephie snorted. "Spill it, Silas. I've been reading your brainwaves for almost a week. Who is it? I know you like her."

"She's some new kid. Her name is Emmeline. She seems kind of nice."

"Seems kind of nice? You've had lunch with her four days in a row. You used to have lunch with us every day."

"I told her I can see ghosts and she's fine with it."

"What else did you tell her? Did you tell her about us? About our powers? About dimensional shifting?"

"Of course not, I just told her you were my friends. She wants to meet you. I'm the only friend she has here. Her parents are divorced and she lives with her mom. I don't know what the deal is with her dad, if she ever sees him."

"Maybe we could all hang out at your house after school and we could meet her."

Sephie rubbed her chin. "Most people aren't fine with ghosts. Do you know why it doesn't bother her?"

"Not really. We haven't talked a lot about that stuff since I first told her. It sounds weird, but I think she has a lot of secrets, the same way we have a lot of secrets. There's something about her. She's different, really different."

Odo grinned. "Silas has a girlfriend, Silas has a–"

Sephie glared at him. "How old are you? Silas met someone he likes, and he's probably not afraid to tell her he likes her."

"What's that supposed to mean?"

Silas held up his hand. "She's not a girlfriend, but I do like her. Did I happen to mention we solved the mystery of Odo's golden pen at lunch yesterday?"

"What do you mean, you solved it?"

"I know what the pen is trying to tell us. Emmeline and I figured it out."

"No way. You told her about the pen?"

Sephie gave a laugh. "I knew it! I knew that's what you were going to do. I knew you were going to ask her to write with the pen."

Odo said, "So what did you figure out? What's the pen for?"

"I'll let Emmeline tell you after school. She's the one who gave me the final clue."

"You're going to make us wait?"

"There's a few things we have to figure out before we tell you. We have to do some research."

Sephie grabbed Odo's arm. "We have to go or we'll be late for class. We'll talk to you after school!"

"See you!"

Silas was sitting with Emmeline at lunch when he spotted Odo and Sephie on the other side of the cafeteria. He decided not to wait until after school. He waved to them, motioning for them to come over.

"Is it okay if Odo and Sephie sit with us?"

"I guess so. They're nice?"

"They're really nice, you'll like them a lot. I'm not sure if you know, but Odo is translucent, really hard to see. He was born that way. It's a long story, but it wasn't an accident. It doesn't bother him anymore, and he actually kind of likes it."

"I wouldn't mind being translucent. People wouldn't stare at me."

Silas wasn't sure what to say, relieved when Odo and Sephie sat down next to them.

"You must be Emmeline. I'm Sephie, and this translucent guy is Odo Whitley, my best friend."

"Hi, Sephie. Hi, Odo. I've never seen a translucent person before."

Silas laughed. "Good one, never seen a translucent person before? That's like the old joke where the invisible man walks into a doctor's office and says–"

Emmeline's face was bright red. "I didn't mean it that way, I meant I've never met a translucent person.

44

I'd never say something like that."

Odo laughed. "I've heard all the jokes, mostly from Silas. Believe it or not, I like being translucent, and the jokes don't bother me at all."

Sephie whispered, "Odo has a special ring he can wear that makes him solid, easy to see."

Emmeline looked dubious. "That sounds a little bit like magic. Or really advanced technology."

Sephie looked at Silas. "You were right, she is smart."

"You said I was smart?"

"I may have said something like that. Anyway, you are smart. You're the one who figured out the secret of the golden pen."

Odo laughed. "That sounds like a book, *Ghostwatcher and the Secret of the Golden Pen.*"

"Who's Ghostwatcher?"

"That's Silas' nickname."

"Because he can see ghosts?"

"Right. We each have a nickname because we each have different stuff we can do."

"What kind of stuff?"

Silas said, "We can talk about all that later. Tell them what we figured out about the pen."

Emmeline said, "Silas said Odo could only write *110,* Sephie could only write *420*, and he could only write *Tectus.* He let me try the pen and I could only write *Street.* It's an address, *110420 Tectus Street.*"

"Whoa, that's amazing. Is it a real place?"

Emmeline nodded. "It's a real place, about three

miles from my house. It's also the house that my mom has been trying to sell. She's a real estate agent."

"No way." Odo glanced at Sephie, raising his eyebrows. "That's a serious connection. A serious one."

Sephie said. "I know. Are you thinking what I'm thinking?"

"I am. You should tell her about the work ring."

Sephie looked at Emmeline. "When Odo found the pen he was wearing a special ring called his work ring. We'll tell you the whole story later, but the ring causes coincidences to occur that show the hidden connections between things that most people aren't aware of."

"What does that mean?"

"The work ring wanted Odo to find the pen and it wanted four people to write with it so we would get the address. You're one of the four people. You're also part of this because you have a direct connection to the house on Tectus Street. Somehow the ring knew that. It wanted us to meet you. We need to understand where the pen came from and why it gave us that address. The first thing we need to do is investigate the house. Do you know anything about it? Who lives there, or who used to live there?"

Emmeline looked at Silas. "Is all this real?"

Silas nodded. "It's very real. This isn't the first time we've done this. Odo and Sephie and I have had some very strange adventures together. One thing I do know is you can trust me, and you can trust them."

Emmeline smiled. "That's actually two things."

Odo snorted. "Nice! You'll fit right in."

Sephie said, "We look out for each other, no matter what."

Emmeline took a deep breath. "I guess I should tell you, my mom said the house at 110420 Tectus Street is haunted."

Chapter 8

Powers

The four friends decided to meet at Silas' house after school, Emmeline's mom happy to hear she had made some friends, ones she really liked. They hopped off the bus a block from his house, laughing at a goofy joke Odo had just made.

Sephie strolled along next to Emmeline, saying, "Does anyone ever call you Emmy, or is it just Emmeline?"

Without thinking, Emmeline answered, "My brother used to call me Emmy."

Sephie's smile faded. "He used to?"

Silas said, "You have a brother?"

She looked away from them. "I don't want to talk about it right now. Sorry."

"That's fine, it's okay."

Silas ran up the steps to their front porch, unlocking the door. "My parents are at work, but my grandma is home. My grandpa is in Africa for a month working on a project."

"What's he doing in Africa?"

"He's an inventor. He's working on a big project that will transform the Sahara Desert into farmland. It's a crazy high tech machine that makes it rain a lot."

Silas called out, "Grandma! We're home! Odo and Sephie and Emmeline are here!"

The woman Silas had once called The Lady in Black stepped out of the kitchen, waving to them. "Hi, Sephie. Hi, Odo." She looked at Emmeline, saying, "And you must be Emmeline. Silas has told me so much about you. He was right, you are beautiful."

A dreadful silence filled the room. Silas wanted to die. He wanted to turn to dust, have the wind carry him into outer space, have aliens blast him into glowing plasma. "Grandma? Really?"

"What?"

Odo and Sephie were grinning, Emmeline was staring at Silas, her jaw hanging open.

"I shouldn't have said that? She is beautiful, Silas, and that's nothing to be embarrassed about."

Silas closed his eyes. "Grandma, do we have any snacks?"

"Of course, I'll run get some." Grandma smiled at Emmeline, whispering, "Sorry if I embarrassed you!"

Silas slumped down in a chair, desperately trying to redirect the conversation. "So you said the house on Tectus Street is haunted?"

Emmeline was still staring at Silas. "Um... my mom said people have seen strange things there, objects floating, moving around by themselves. Someone saw a bicycle floating across the front porch. And they heard loud crashing noises from inside the house. A window broke once, an alarm clock flying out of the house, landing in the neighbor's yard."

"Whoa." Odo turned to Silas. "Does that sound like a ghost? Can ghosts move stuff? I thought they couldn't interact with the physical world?"

"It doesn't sound like any ghost I've ever seen."

Sephie said, "It sounds like someone with powers lived there."

Emmeline looked puzzled. "What kind of powers?"

"Show her."

Sephie held out her hand, drawing a symbol in the air. Emmeline gave a shriek when a book floated up from the table, drifting around the room. "What's happening? How are you doing that?"

The book landed gently on the kitchen counter.

"It's one of my powers. I'm half Fortisian and half human. My mom was human, my dad was from Fortisia. They both died when I was a baby."

"What's Fortisia?"

"It's a distant world where people have powers like mine. Full blooded Fortisians have incredible powers. I can move objects using my mind, I can read people's brainwaves, and I can control their thoughts, make them see things that aren't really there, implant memories that never actually happened. Things like that."

Emmeline looked around to see if the others were laughing. They weren't. "You're saying you could make me see something that's not there? Like a green cat? That's not possible."

She gave a yelp when she saw the bright green cat strolling across the carpet. "No way. Is that real?"

"It's not real. I'm sending electrical signals to your visual cortex, the same signals your optic nerve would send it if you were really seeing a green cat."

Odo said, "Her nickname is Encephalo Girl. That's what the doctors called her when she was little. She can see people's brain waves, like an encephalogram, see what parts of their brain are active. If you know about brain mapping, you can tell a lot about what they're thinking, if they're happy or sad or scared or angry. They shortened Encephalo Girl to Sephie. That's how she got her name.

Emmeline was gaping at Sephie. "You're an alien?"

"I guess you could say that, but someone from another planet would say all of us were aliens."

"That's true. Wait, is that why your hair is so orange?"

"Exactly. I'm impressed."

"Thanks. What's Odo's nickname?"

"Not a big surprise, but I'm the Translucent Boy. Someone named Wikerus Praevian altered my DNA before I was born and made me translucent. Being translucent makes it hard for people to see me, but it also lets me to do something called dimensional shifting."

"What's that?"

"It means I can travel to other worlds and other

dimensions using a waystone. A waystone is an object that comes from the other world or dimension."

"You're saying if you had a rock from Mars, you could travel there?"

"Correct, but I wouldn't want to go because there's no breathable air. You have to be very careful with waystones, some of them can take you into deadly environments."

Emmeline leaned back in her chair, her eyes on Odo. "You visit other worlds, worlds that aren't like this one, worlds with alien creatures?" Her eyes were bright.

Sephie was studying her brain waves. This was interesting.

"Exactly, I can travel there using waystones."

Emmeline asked, "Can you fly when you're there?"

"Some of them have antigravity cars and interstellar ships. Is that what you mean?"

"Not exactly. I was wondering if you had any powers there that you don't have here, like flying."

Sephie could see that Emmeline was hiding something. Silas had been right, she had a lot of secrets.

"I'm solid in other worlds, but I don't have any special powers there."

Emmeline said, "There's something I have to tell you. Some things about me that you should know."

Chapter 9

Ex Cineribus Resurgam

Emmeline's voice was shaking. Revealing the deep secrets of her life was the hardest and scariest thing she'd ever done. They would know, they would judge. She looked at Silas, then began.

"I didn't have a very happy life when I was a kid. My dad drank a lot and my mom and him would fight. Sometimes he'd yell at us and say mean things, bad things, sometimes he'd start crying and say how sorry he was, that he'd never drink again. I never knew what he would be like when I came home from school. I hated opening the front door."

"Your dad was an alcoholic?"

Emmeline nodded. "When I was eight years old he told us to get in the car, that he was taking us all to the movies. He'd been drinking. My mom thought the movie was too old for us, but my dad said it was fine. She said she should drive, but he got mad, said he was fine. I was sitting in the back seat of the car with my brother Jacob. My mom and dad were in the front seat."

Silas' heart sank when he saw Ghost Boy appear next to Emmeline, his hand on her shoulder. A wave of deep sadness rolled through him. He knew Ghost Boy was Jacob. He knew how Emmeline's story was going to end, and it wasn't going to be good.

"My mom and dad started fighting about the movie on the way there. My mom thought we should see a different one. I was crying and Jacob leaned over, whispering, 'It's okay, Emmy, everything will be okay.' He used to say that to me a lot, except this time it wasn't okay.

"The driver in front of us jammed on his brakes to avoid a dog that ran into the street. My dad was yelling at my mom and didn't notice until it was too late. He swerved, and our car skidded, rolling over and over and over down a ravine. I was unconscious for almost two days, and Jacob died. My mom and dad got divorced after that and he left. I haven't seen my dad since then. My legs were all messed up in the accident. I had really bad multiple compound fractures. They did the best they could but we didn't have much money, and our insurance wouldn't pay for it. That's why I walk the way I do."

The room was silent, all eyes on Emmeline.

Silas said, "I'm so sorry. I had no idea."

Sephie gave Emmeline a hug. "You are so brave to tell us all that. It must have been so hard for you and your mom."

"It was. There's more though. It's hard to talk about

it. I don't want you to think I'm crazy."

"You can tell us anything. It's okay, I promise."

Emmeline told them the story of how she had created the Cube, her safe place in the world of dreams. How she had visited dozens of dream worlds, worlds where she was safe, where her legs were straight, where nothing could hurt her, where she could fly.

"That's why you asked me if I could fly in other worlds?"

Emmeline nodded.

"Are you sure the worlds you visit are dream worlds and not real worlds? They sound pretty real. There are people who can send their consciousness to other worlds. It's a power called the Traveling Eye." He didn't mention that Sephie was one of those people.

"I can't fly in the real world. I've tried a thousand times here and can't do it."

Sephie said, "There are some Fortisians who can fly. It's the same principle as when I made the book float across the room, but a lot harder to do. They have to go through years of training."

Ghost Boy was looking at Silas, the metal spike still clutched in his hand. Silas sent him a thought. *I can't tell her about you with everyone here. I promise I'll tell her later."*

The ghost nodded, then vanished.

Emmeline said, "That's everything. I've never told anyone about any of this before, not about my dad drinking and especially not about the Cube. I haven't had a normal fun life."

Sephie said, "My mom and dad died when I was little. They were killed by alien beings called Stirpians. My parents had something the Stirpians wanted, something they needed to invade our home planet, Fortisia. They didn't get it, my mom and dad dying to protect our world. I didn't learn about any of that until last year. I thought I was just a weird orphan with crazy orange hair. For most of my childhood I thought my parents gave me up because they didn't want me. Our friend Wikerus Praevian told me all about it. He'd been looking for me since my parents died."

Odo said, "I spent my whole childhood being lonely because no one ever saw me. Even my parents had a hard time seeing me. They still do. Wikerus Praevian saw me, but Sephie was the first person to really, really see me. She was my first real friend. She also said something I will never forget."

Silas said, "What?"

"*Ex cineribus resurgam.*"

"That doesn't exactly sound like something I'd never forget."

"It means, *Out of the ashes I shall rise.*"

"You mean going through all this hard stuff makes us stronger?"

Sephie nodded. "Some people call the trials we face the fires of life."

Odo raised his hand. "A little off topic, but didn't your grandma mention something about snacks?"

"What's wrong with you, Odo Whitley? We're having a serious talk about our lives."

"That's what's making me so hungry."

Emmeline burst out laughing.

It was the first time Silas had seen her laugh.

The conversation turned to less serious matters, Silas' grandma bringing in a tray of cookies. When they were done eating, Silas took them down to the basement and showed them his grandpa's workshop and a few of the incredible devices he had invented, including his Ghostwatcher glasses that allowed the viewer to see other worlds and dimensions.

"He was trying to make glasses that would let people see ghosts like he did, but he accidentally invented glasses that let you see other dimensions, other worlds."

Emmeline said, "Are they like virtual reality goggles?"

Silas shook his head. "No, you're actually looking at real worlds, not digital ones. These places really exist, and you're looking at them."

"Can I try it?"

"Sure. I'll find a good one." He called out, "Hey, Watson, what's the code for that world with all the beautiful flowers and trees? The one with the cool old temples?"

"One moment, Silas, while I search the database."

Emmeline whispered, "Who is that? Is that your grandpa?"

"No, it's an engineered intelligence he scavenged off a damaged Atroxian android. I call him Watson because he's like Alexander Graham Bell's assistant."

Emmeline stared at Silas. "You're not joking?"

"I'm not. It's what I was trying to tell you before. The universe is a very big and very complex place, full of different worlds and dimensions and trillions of different life forms."

"Silas, the world you seek is 259.2 Alpha G."

"Thanks, Watson." Silas picked up a pair of glasses from the cluttered workbench, tapping them, a holographic screen appearing. He entered the location code into a grid of numbers and letters, then handed the glasses to Emmeline.

Emmeline let out a low gasp when she put them on. "This is incredible. It's so beautiful. It looks so real, like I could reach out and touch it. The temples look like they're made of white shimmering glass, and the carved figures are amazing. They look a little like us. All those flowers and trees, it's so beautiful. And the pink sky is amazing. Do people live here?"

Silas shook his head. "Not anymore. Watson said there was a gigantic war a few thousand years ago and they were all wiped out. They had super advanced technology but it didn't do them much good. They're not the first race to destroy themselves."

Emmeline took off the glasses, handing them to Silas. "Your grandpa must be a genius."

Silas nodded. "He is. He's taught me a lot of stuff about alien technology. It's all secret though, not stuff this world is ready for. He said we'd destroy ourselves if we had it since we're such primitive beings."

"I can't believe I thought you might be the kind of person who would laugh at me."

"I would never do that."

Odo said, "Sephie laughs at me all the time. It's not so bad."

Sephie gave him a sweet smile. "I'm not laughing *at* you, Odo Whitley, I'm laughing at your endless stream of hilarious jokes."

Silas snorted.

Odo said, "Okay, time to get serious. Emmeline, is there any way you can get us into the house on Tectus Street?"

She pulled a slip of paper from her pocket. "Funny you should mention that. This is the code to the lock box."

"Perfect. How about Saturday morning? We can check it out, maybe find some clues about the golden pen and who owned it."

Chapter 10

110420 Tectus Street

Saturday morning found the four friends gathered outside the mysterious gray house on Tectus Street.

"It looks like a normal house, not spooky like Wikerus Praevian's house."

"He lives in an old Victorian mansion. They all look haunted."

"So we just go in?"

"That's the plan." Emmeline stepped up onto the porch. She pointed to a window well, the mud spattered glass protected by heavy wrought iron bars. "It has a basement. It looks a bit scary down there."

"Odo, why don't you go down and see what's making those weird scratching noises."

Sephie laughed.

"Very funny. We have one rule today; we don't split up to investigate the basement or the attic. Oh, second rule, if we see someone with a chainsaw we leave immediately."

"Good plan."

Emmeline removed the lockbox key, opening the

front door. "In we go." She stepped inside the house.

"It's totally empty, no furniture. This doesn't look too promising for clues."

Sephie grabbed Odo's arm, her voice low and whispery. "Maybe we'll find something in the basement."

Odo rolled his eyes. "You guys are not scaring me at all. Nothing scares the amazing Translucent Boy."

Silas said, "Here's the kitchen. Nothing weird here, it looks like a normal kitchen." He pulled open a few drawers. "Empty."

Emmeline opened the lower cabinet doors. "Sometimes things fall down below and people can't see if— ha!"

"What is it?"

"A spoon in the back corner." She kneeled down, reaching in and pulling it out. "It's sterling silver."

Sephie said, "And it has a monogram on it."

"GMB, the same initials as the gold pen."

"So whoever owned the pen lived here. That's a really important clue."

"Do you think we're supposed to return the pen to its original owner?"

"I don't know."

The friends searched the house thoroughly, including the attic and the basement, finding nothing of interest except the silver monogrammed spoon.

"Emmeline, did your mom say who owned the house?"

"She didn't. I can check it out though, she has a folder for each of her listings. It should be in there."

"Nice. We should get going. I have to help my dad clean the garage. What could be more fun than that?"

Silas nodded. "I'm going to walk Emmeline home."

Sephie gave a dramatic sigh. "Odo never walks me home."

"Fine, I'll walk you home. You can use your crazy powers to protect us if we get attacked by alien assassins."

"Odo the Brave, my hero."

Silas and Emmeline headed down Tectus Street toward Expergo Street, Silas saying, "Our friend Wikerus Praevian lives on the same street you do. We go past his house on the way to yours."

"You can call me Emmy if you want."

"Okay, thanks." Silas grinned.

"Do you think it's weird that I created the Cube?"

"It's not weird at all, it's amazing that you could do it. Um, there's something I need to tell you, but it might kind of freak you out. Maybe a lot."

Emmy stopped, concern on her face. "What kind of something? Is it something I said?"

"It's not about you, it's about ghosts, and one ghost in particular I've been seeing since I first saw you on the school bus."

Emmy froze. "No."

Silas said, "I promised him I would tell you I saw him. It's Jacob, and I see him a lot. He's around you a lot."

Emmy's eyes welled up with tears. "You really see him? You see Jacob? You see him?"

"He was standing next to you when you were telling us about the accident. His hand was on your shoulder. I knew how your story was going to end."

She wiped her eyes. "You can talk to him?"

"Sometimes ghosts talk and sometimes they don't. Jacob can hear my thoughts, but I can't hear his. I don't really know how that works. I told you I could see ghosts because he wanted me to tell you. I didn't know it was Jacob then, I just called him Ghost Boy. I didn't know who he was until today."

"What does he look like? Is he... hurt... from the accident?"

"No, he's fine. He looks about the same age he was when he passed on. His physical earthly body was damaged, not his spectral body."

"I don't know what that means."

"Ghosts have a spectral body they create with their mind. That's what I see, not the physical body they used to have. It's a little like the body you create for yourself when you have a dream."

"He didn't have any messages for me?"

"He doesn't talk to me, just kind of points at stuff. It's like playing charades, you have to sort of guess what it means. There's one thing that's confusing to me. He had something in his hand he kept showing me. It looked like a black metal spike about seven inches long. Does that mean anything to you?"

"A metal spike? He never had anything like that. I have no idea what it is."

"It might be something he wants us to find, or it

might symbolize something. We'll figure it out."

"Is that Wikerus Praevian's house? It really does look haunted. Sephie said he's a Fortisian?"

"That's his spooky house. He's a Fortisian, and also a formshifter, can change his appearance. He looks like an old man with white hair, but he's actually about as old as my dad and has bright orange hair like Sephie. All Fortisians have the same orange hair. His assistant is Mrs. Preke. She looks like a frumpy old lady, but she's a Plindorian, also a formshifter."

"What's a Plindorian?"

"You'd totally freak out if you saw her. She's a giant yellow octopus."

Emmy laughed. "You sound like Odo."

"It's true, Plindorians look like big yellow octopuses, but they're really smart. Odo and Sephie have been to Plindor and seen them."

"It's so hard to believe all this is real."

"You get used to it and it all just seems normal. It's just the way the world is, nothing weird about it."

Emmy stopped, taking Silas' hand. "Thanks for telling me about Jacob. When you first told me you could talk to ghosts I was hoping maybe you could talk to him, but I was kind of afraid to ask you."

"I know it can be kind of scary to think about. Jacob is a ghost, but he's still Jacob, no different than he was."

"That thing your grandma said about me. Did you really tell her that?"

Silas nodded. "I did."

Chapter 11

221 B

Odo crawled out of bed, heading down to breakfast. He'd gotten an email from Emmy saying she had the name of the person who used to live in the house on Tectus Street. The only problem was that the owner, Mrs. Evelyn Bailey, was currently residing at the Shady Pines Retirement Facility, thirty-four miles from Odo's house.

Odo stepped into the kitchen, announcing his arrival.

"Odo Whitley is in the house! All hail King Odo!"

Albert, Odo's dad, glared at him over his newspaper. "I can't read the paper with all that racket. Walk into a room like a normal person. And just to be clear, you're not King Odo."

"Remember the time I walked in when you and Mom were fighting and you didn't know I was there?"

"We weren't fighting, we were having a loud discussion."

Petunia, Odo's Mom, nodded her head. "It's true,

your father and I never fight."

"Right. Are you going to that new store today, None of Odo's Business?" Odo's grin faded when he saw the look of panic on his mom's face.

Albert lowered his paper. "What on earth are you talking about? There's no such store as that, everyone knows that."

"Just kidding. Just another one of my hilarious jokes."

Albert looked over his glasses at Odo. "Just because something is ridiculous doesn't mean it's funny. It's also not funny if no one knows what you're talking about."

His mom's panicked expression had disappeared. Clearly she didn't want Albert to know where she was going. That was odd. Odo couldn't imagine his mom having secrets.

She gave him a bright smile. "How about some delicious waffles for breakfast, King Odo?"

"Sounds good."

Albert stood up. "Don't encourage his silly behavior. The world isn't a silly place. Time for work. We're launching the new advertising campaign for Golden CrunchCake Delights today. I have lots to do. I'll be home late."

Odo said, "They sound really good. Hope you sell a lot."

Albert nodded. "They are good, they have a creamy crunch chocolate flavored filling. I'll bring a few boxes home. You can share them with your friends. Word of mouth is the best kind of advertising."

"Great, thanks." He groaned to himself. He'd rather eat a bag of sawdust.

Ten minutes after Albert left, his mom said, "I have to go. Have a good day at school." She gave him a hug, whispering, "Thanks, King Odo."

The bus wouldn't be there for another half hour, so Odo decided to call the Shady Pines Retirement Facility and talk to Mrs. Bailey, see if she knew anything about the gold pen. He dialed the number, taking a seat at the kitchen table.

"Shady Pines Retirement Facility, how may I help you?"

"Hi, can I talk to Mrs. Evelyn Bailey, please?"

"Who is calling?"

"Just a friend calling to say hello."

"I'm afraid Mrs. Bailey isn't taking calls."

"When would be a good time to call?"

"Perhaps I wasn't clear. She's not taking any phone calls. It's very upsetting to her, she can become quite agitated. Perhaps you could just send her a nice card, something pleasant."

"When are your visiting hours?"

"I'm afraid Mrs. Bailey isn't taking any visitors at this time either. It's far too unsettling for her. It's best if you send a nice card, maybe something with flowers on it."

"Right." Odo's mind was racing. This lady was definitely hiding something.

"I'm afraid I have another call. Have a lovely day,

and thank you for calling Shady Pines." There were three loud clicks on the line when she hung up.

Odo stared at the phone. That was totally weird. What were those clicks? Was someone else listening? They didn't want anyone talking to Mrs. Bailey, but why?

The four friends met at lunch in the cafeteria, Odo telling them about the odd phone call to the Shady Pines Retirement Facility.

Silas nudged Emmy. "Something shady is going on there."

"What do you mean?" She blinked her eyes at him.

"Something shady? At Shady Pines?"

"I got it, just kidding."

Odo snorted. "Quit stealing my jokes."

Sephie said, "What are we going to do?"

"We have to talk to Mrs. Bailey. The lady I called was definitely hiding something, didn't want anyone to talk to her. Maybe she's being held there against her will. She could be a prisoner."

"Or she could be suffering from dementia."

"No, this lady was acting really suspiciously. Maybe we could go there and you could scan her brain waves."

"That wouldn't tell us much, just that she's hiding something."

"We could sneak in and talk to Mrs. Bailey."

"I have a better idea. I'll use the Traveling Eye to check out the place. I'll find Mrs. Bailey's room and see what's going on."

Emmy said, "How does the Traveling Eye work

exactly?"

"I can send my consciousness somewhere else, see and hear everything there, but they can't see me. It's a little like being a ghost."

Odo said, "She can fly through walls, so locked doors aren't a problem."

"I can't talk to anyone though, and they can't see me."

"At least we'll know if she's a prisoner. If she is, maybe you can learn why."

"I'll do it after school and let you know what I find out."

That evening after dinner, Odo got a call from Sephie.

"You were right, there's something strange going on at Shady Pines."

"What happened? What did you see?"

"I found the building and flew into the reception area. A nurse was talking on the phone at the front desk, telling someone there hadn't been any changes with Mrs. Bailey, that she still wasn't telling them anything about what had happened. She said they would keep trying, that Mrs. Bailey knew a lot more than she was saying."

"Did she say what it was that happened?"

"No, but I saw the room directory and found Mrs. Bailey's room. She's in room 221B. I flew up to the second floor and found it. There were two armed guards in black uniforms outside her door."

"Why would she have guards?"

"I don't know, but it gets even stranger."

"Like what?"

"I went into her room and saw her. She's old and has white hair. She was sleeping in her bed. I didn't see any personal items there, no photos or books."

"That is strange."

"That's not the strange part."

"What happened?"

"When I was looking at her, she opened her eyes and said hello."

"She could see you? That's not possible, you're like a ghost."

"And yet it happened, Odo Whitley. She looked directly at me, smiled, and said how nice it was to have a visitor. We have to go see her, talk to her. There's a lot more going on here than we thought, and Mrs. Evelyn Bailey is not at all what she appears to be."

Chapter 12

Mrs. Bailey

After school, Odo and Sephie rode the city bus to the Shady Pines Retirement Facility.

Odo peered through the tall wrought iron spiked fence that surrounded Shady Pines. "This place is kind of spooky. Why do they need a giant fence like this?"

"To keep people out?"

"Or to keep people in."

They slipped through the front gate, walking down the long curving walkway across the meticulously manicured grounds of the facility.

"This place looks like a billionaire's private mansion. It must be super expensive to live here."

"Unless you're being held prisoner."

"Check out those three big black cars with the weird antennas parked under the trees. Nothing suspicious about that. Too bad Silas and Emmy couldn't be here."

"This is a stealth mission, Odo Whitley, not a picnic."

"So I shouldn't have brought the checkered table-cloth and the potato salad?"

"Very funny. There's the front entrance."

"We just walk in?"

Sephie stared at him. "Stealth mission?"

"What's the plan?"

"We peek through the window and see if anyone is at the reception desk."

The two friends walked quickly to the front door. Sephie peered in, then ducked back out of view. "There's a nurse there, and she doesn't look friendly. She's probably the one you talked to."

"What are you going to do?"

"I'm going to manipulate her thoughts, implant a false memory."

"What kind of memory?"

Sephie drew three symbols in the air. "She just remembered she forgot to lock her car in the back parking lot, and she left her phone on the front seat."

Sephie stood up and peeked through the window again. "She's gone, let's roll. It's showtime, Odo Whitley."

"Why don't I get to say cool stuff like that?"

"You can say whatever you want. You could say, let's rock and roll, that would be appropriate."

"It's too late now, it would just sound dumb. You already said let's roll and it's showtime. Anything I said at this point would be redundant, not cool at all, like I was just copying what you were saying."

"Okay, fine. Next time you can say it." Sephie pulled the front door open, heading inside. "The stairs are over there."

They darted past the reception area and up the stairway, Sephie whispering, "Keep your eyes open for guards."

"Just so you're aware, you said two cool things back there, let's roll and it's showtime. You should only be allowed one catchphrase. That should be our new rule, one catchphrase per superhero."

"What's wrong with your brain? We're on a secret stealth mission. Focus, it doesn't matter who says what. Let's roll, boys."

Odo glared at her. "That's not your catchphrase."

Sephie peered through the small window at the top of the stairs. "Two armed guards in chairs outside her room. I'll wait here while you go in and clobber them."

"What?"

"Just seeing if you were paying attention. Time for a little mind manipulation. The guards are getting very, very sleepy."

Odo looked through the window, watching the guards slump over in their chairs, their eyes closed.

Sephie studied the guards. "We're good."

Odo swung the door open. "It's showtime."

"I already said it was showtime, Odo Whitley. It can't be more showtime than it already is."

"Fine."

The two friends darted down the hallway, Odo's eyes on the sleeping guards. He pointed to an embroidered patch on the guard's shoulder. "What does XODC mean?"

Sephie shrugged, trying the door. "Her door's locked."

Odo pressed his hand against the door. Ten seconds later they stepped through a shimmering translucent rectangle into Mrs. Bailey's room.

Odo stopped short, eyeing the old woman in the flowery robe sitting in a chair next to the window. She turned, smiling at them. "Hello, again, young lady. It's so lovely to have visitors."

Sephie gave a bright smile. "I'm Sephie, and this is my friend Odo. You're Mrs. Bailey?"

"I am indeed. Is Odo your boyfriend? He's quite handsome, isn't he? You're not a movie star, are you, young man?"

"Um... no. You can see me?"

"Of course, dear. I might be old but I can still see."

"Right, it's just that I'm..."

"You're not the first translucent person I've seen, you know."

Sephie said, "Who are you, exactly?"

"I'm Mrs. Evelyn Bailey. I thought you already knew that? Isn't that why you're here? To see me?"

"Why are there armed guards outside your door? Why wouldn't they let us talk to you? They said it would be too upsetting for you."

"Do I look upset?"

"Not even a little."

Mrs. Bailey stood up, her eyes on Odo. It felt like

ants were marching around in his head. She smiled, turning to Sephie. "Your boyfriend is true, just like my George."

Sephie looked puzzled. "He's true?"

Mrs. Bailey said, "Yes, he is. That's a very good thing to be."

Odo pulled the golden pen from his pocket, showing it to Mrs. Bailey.

"You found George's pen! How marvelous. He would have been so happy."

"George was your husband?"

"Indeed, he was. A lovely man, the love of my life."

"We had some questions about the pen."

Mrs. Bailey smiled. "I imagine so."

"Do you know anything about it?"

Mrs. Bailey took a seat, eyeing Sephie. "I'm parched. Doesn't a nice glass of cold water sound lovely?" She looked around the room, then said, "Oh dear, there doesn't seem to be any water."

Sephie's eyes narrowed. What game was she playing?

Mrs. Bailey drew a symbol in the air, a glass of water appearing on the table next to her in a flash of blue light.

Sephie took a step back. "You're a Fortisian!"

"I used to have lovely orange hair just like yours."

"You know what I am?

"Of course I do, sweetie. What I don't know is why you're here."

Odo's eyes were on the glass of water. "Why are you

being held prisoner?"

"I am here due to a rather unfortunate condition of mine. Some people sleepwalk, I levitate objects in my sleep. George could never get used to seeing objects floating around the room while I was sleeping."

"That's why they said your house was haunted. Someone saw a bicycle floating across the front porch."

Mrs. Bailey laughed. "I was taking a nap on the couch when that happened. A few days later I started seeing mysterious black cars parked outside my house, those silly XODC people spying on me."

"Who are they?"

"Some ridiculous secret branch of the government trying to protect the world from aliens. They call themselves the Exo Defense Command. Can you imagine, grown men locking up a little old lady for levitating objects in her sleep? They don't have the slightest idea about the true nature of this universe. If they did, they wouldn't be worried about someone like me."

"You could leave Shady Pines anytime you want. You have the power to do that."

"Of course I could, dearie, but I'm old, and I find all their silly questions strangely entertaining, more fun than watching TV. I pretend I don't know anything, but also act as though I'm hiding something. It annoys them dreadfully. It's hard not to laugh when they ask such ridiculous questions."

Odo said, "Can't you make them forget about you? Cloud their thoughts like Sephie does?"

"That's precisely what I'll do when I grow tired of them."

"What do you know about the pen?"

"It's an artifact from Fortisia that I gave George for his birthday. The pens were quite a fad there about a hundred years ago. They're like a cosmic to-do list, using the power of synchronicity to guide you. They're great fun, but the messages are annoyingly vague, often difficult to understand. It operates under the same principles as your work ring, Odo."

Odo blinked. "How could you possibly know about that?"

Chapter 13

The Hidden Room

Mrs. Bailey winked at Sephie. "He's so cute. How could I possibly know that. Such a dear."

"She read your thoughts and memories, Odo Whitley."

"That's what that was? It felt like ants walking around in my head."

Mrs. Bailey said, "Okay, kiddos, let's get to it. Odo is wondering what George's pen had to do with his vision of the old man in the boat who tried to drown him. I don't have an answer for you, but it's very clear the pen led you to me. What I can tell you is that George had a large collection of alien artifacts hidden in our basement. I never paid much attention to them, but we did have great fun playing with the pen for a while. May I borrow it for a moment, Odo?"

"Of course, it's your pen." He handed the pen to Mrs. Bailey.

There was a flash of light and a piece of paper appeared on the table. Mrs. Bailey turned, writing something on the paper.

"Very interesting, indeed. A tantalizing clue to your thrilling mystery." She handed Odo the paper. He read it out loud.

"Odysseus."

"Isn't that interesting? The mystery you're trying to solve must have something to do with Greek mythology, Odysseus, and the wooden boat you saw."

"I guess that helps a little. Wait, what happened to all the alien artifacts? Are they still in the basement?"

"I haven't been in the secret room since George sold the collection to a Fortisian collector, but there might be a few artifacts left." She stopped, frowning. "I'm remembering something. I think he may have had an object that came from an old boat, a mythological one. Many of those old myths do have some basis in fact, you know."

"Would you mind if we looked in the secret room?"

"I wouldn't mind at all, dear." She waved Odo over to her, taking his hand in hers, whispering, "I know you will have a wonderful life with your dear friend Sephie, just as George and I did. I gave this to George, and now I'm giving it to you."

"Really? That's so nice of you. Thanks."

Sephie turned when she heard the doorknob rattle, someone inserting a key. Mrs. Bailey drew a quick symbol, a voice calling out, "The key broke off in the lock. We need to get this door open!"

There was a loud knock on the door. "Mrs. Bailey, is

there someone in there with you?"

Odo whispered, "It's that crazy nurse!"

Mrs. Bailey laughed. "Isn't she dreadful? She really should be in a scary movie, skulking about in the night."

"Is there another way out of here? Does the window open?"

Sephie said, "I can make them forget everything."

Mrs. Bailey smiled. "What fun would that be? Hold on, I'll help you. You will come back and visit me again?"

Sephie gave her a hug. "Of course we will. Thank you so much for the pen."

"You're very welcome, dear. Now, off you go!"

She drew four symbols, Odo and Sephie vanishing in a blink of light.

A split second later they appeared on the sidewalk in front of Odo's house.

"Whoa! That was incredible! How did she do that?"

"She blinked us here. Cyra was trying to teach me how to do that on Plindor, but I never could get it right. Don't forget, Mrs. Bailey is a full blooded Fortisian, just like Cyra."

"Sweet, we saved six dollars on the bus fare. Ka-ching!"

Sephie stared at Odo.

"What?"

"Nothing. We need to meet Silas and Emmy at Mrs. Bailey's house and check out the hidden room.

Odo raised one eyebrow, his voice low and gravelly.

"Let's do this thing."

"That doesn't work, Odo Whitley. You have to say it right before you do the thing or it doesn't make sense. You can't say let's do this thing, and then do it three days later."

"I thought it worked okay, but I probably should have used my normal voice. Let's call Silas and Emmy, have them meet us at the house on Tectus Street."

The four friends met outside Mrs. Bailey's house, Odo recounting in great detail their meeting with her at Shady Pines.

"She's a Fortisian?"

"She is. I'm not sure if her husband was, but she definitely is. She has amazing powers. She blinked us to my house from Shady Pines."

Emmy unlocked the front door and they stepped inside, then headed down the stairs, Odo flipping the lights on.

"Now we just have to find the hidden room." He pressed his hand against the wall, peering through the translucent circle that formed, moving slowly down the length of the room, stopping abruptly. "Got it! There's an armored door behind this wall panel."

Emmy said, "How do we open an armored door?"

"We don't, we walk right through it." The circle around Odo's hand grew until it formed a shimmering six foot tall rectangle. "We're good. Let's roll."

Sephie nodded. "That worked well, very appropriate."

The four friends stepped into the hidden room.

Sephie flicked her hand and a ball of light appeared in front of her, illuminating the room.

Emmy jumped back. "What is that thing?"

"Oh, sorry. I'm manipulating energy, creating a sphere of electromagnetic radiation in the visible light spectrum."

"Radiation? Isn't that dangerous?"

Odo said, "She made a ball of light so we can see. Light is electromagnetic radiation, not dangerous at all."

Emmy stared at Sephie. "That's amazing."

"It's just science."

Silas ran over to a light switch, flipping it on. "This works too, and you don't need cool powers."

"The shelves are empty, everything is gone."

"Not everything." Sephie pointed to a nine-inch crystal cube on one of the upper shelves.

"What is that?" Odo darted across the room, reaching up and grabbing the cube. "There's something inside it."

A chill shot through Silas when he saw the seven-inch black metal spike inside the cube.

Emmy said, "Silas, didn't you ask me about a black spike that Jacob had?"

Sephie and Odo both looked at him. "You knew about this? About a black metal spike?"

"I already told Emmy, but the first time I saw her, the ghost of her brother Jacob was there. I've seen him a lot since then. He had something in his hand, something he keeps showing me."

"The black spike?"

Silas nodded. "At first I thought it was a weapon, but now I don't. It looks more like a giant iron nail."

"Why would it be inside this crystal cube?"

Odo set the cube down, saying, "Sephie, touch the cube."

She pressed her hand against it, pulling it away. "It's a waystone. It tingles, even through the crystal."

Silas studied the spike. "It's from another world?"

"Yes. When Odo or I touch a waystone, an electric shock runs through us, sometimes a tingle, sometimes a lot stronger."

Emmy said, "Could you use your dimensional shifting powers to travel to the world where the spike came from?"

"We can, but we're not going to. Not yet, anyway. Not until we find out what kind of world it is. It could have a deadly poisonous atmosphere."

Odo said, "I could reach inside the cube and take the spike out."

"Too dangerous. Wikerus said some waystones are so powerful that just touching them will send you to another world, maybe a deadly one."

"So how do we figure out where it's from?"

Emmy picked up the cube, studying the spike. "There must be some reason Jacob was showing you this. Either he wants us to find it, or he was warning us about it." She turned the cube over, giving a start. "There's a card taped to the bottom!" She gently peeled it off, showing it to them.

Professor Otto Liedenbrock
Archeological Mythologist
Berlin

Sephie stared at the old sepia tone card.

"Who in the world is Professor Otto Liedenbrock of Berlin, and what does he have to do with the metal spike?"

Chapter 14

Wikerus

Odo said, "I've never heard of him, but the card is old, like those calling cards they used before people had phones. If someone came to see you but you weren't home, they would leave their calling card."

"Why would an old fashioned calling card be taped to the cube?"

"Maybe George Bailey bought the spike from Otto Liedenbrock?"

"That's not possible. The calling card is at least a hundred years old. No way could George have bought it from Professor Liedenbrock."

Sephie held the card up, examining it. "Unless…"

"Unless what?"

"Unless George and Evelyn Bailey are a lot older than we think they are."

"How long do Fortisians live? Maybe George was a Fortisian."

"We have to go ask Wikerus, but I think they live a

lot longer than humans do. We can ask him about the spike."

"I'll research Professor Liedenbrock online."

Odo said, "Let's think about this first. We know all these weird events are connected; my vision of the crazy old guy in the boat, the spike that Jacob showed me, and now Professor Otto Liedenbrock, Archeological Mythologist."

"What does that mean exactly? What's an archeological mythologist?"

"Good question. I guess it's someone who studies archeology and mythology."

"But mythological stuff isn't real, it's just stories made up by ancient civilizations to explain science that they didn't understand. Like Zeus throwing lightning bolts. They didn't know what electricity was, so they invented a god named Zeus who threw lightning bolts."

"True, but remember what Mrs. Bailey said? She said some of the old myths have a basis in fact. She wrote Odysseus with the pen and said the spike must have something to do with Greek mythology."

Silas' eyes were focused on the metal spike. "Maybe Otto Liedenbrock collected artifacts from mythological tales that were real, not fiction."

"And the metal spike is one of those artifacts."

Odo pressed his hand to his forehead. "I bet the spike is from the wooden boat in my vision! Mrs. Bailey said George had an object from an old mythological boat."

The four friends stared at the metal spike.

"This is amazing, but what does it mean? Why should we care about a big nail from an old boat?"

Emmy said, "We need to research mythological boats, try to identify the one in Odo's vision. Let's look for any boats in Greek mythology that have a connection to Odysseus."

Odo said, "Or we could use the spike as a waystone and go see where it came from."

Sephie shook her head. "Wrong. We need to have a lot more information before we do that."

Silas said, "Let's split up into two teams. Emmy wants to meet Wikerus and Mrs. Preke, so maybe she and Sephie can go see them while Odo and I research Professor Liedenbrock, mythological boats, and Odysseus."

Emmy grinned. "I can't wait to meet them."

They exited the house, Sephie and Emmy heading for Wikerus' house on Expergo Street.

Emmy said, "I walked past his house with Silas. It really does look haunted."

Sephie laughed. "Wikerus and Mrs. Preke are both really nice. The first time Odo and I went there I asked Wikerus if his house was haunted and he said no."

The two friends darted up the steps, the front door opening just as Sephie was about to knock.

Emmy stopped short, her eyes on the open door.

Wikerus stepped out from behind it, a broad smile on his face.

Emmy studied his old fashioned gray suit and snow white hair, the small yellow flower tucked into his lapel. She decided she liked him, he looked like a nice old grandpa.

Wikerus said, "Hello, Sephie. I'd say this was a lovely surprise, but that wouldn't be one hundred percent true. Mrs. Preke said she had a strong feeling you and a new friend would be joining us today." He turned to Emmy with a smile. "Good afternoon, young lady, I'm Wikerus Praevian, and it is my great and profound pleasure to meet you." He tipped his hat politely, giving a slight bow.

"Um, it's so nice to meet you too. Silas told me a lot about you and Mrs. Preke."

"Excellent. Please come in, we can talk in the sitting room. Mrs. Preke is elsewhere I'm afraid, otherwise occupied, but perhaps you can meet her on your next visit."

They followed Wikerus down a wide hallway lined with heavy maroon carpeting to a magnificent sitting room filled with elaborately carved tables and chairs, the walls adorned with marvelous old oil paintings and tapestries.

Emmy took a seat on an exquisitely embroidered blue couch. She had never seen a room like this before. "This is amazing. It's like a dream."

Wikerus sat in a comfortable stuffed mahogany chair, his eyes on Emmy. Her comment seemed to amuse him. "Yes, like a dream. Precisely so." He drew a symbol in the air, a gold box of chocolates appearing on the coffee table. "Chocolates anyone? They're quite good." He plucked one out. "I favor the lemon cremes.

Very tasty."

Emmy's hand hovered over the box. "They're okay to eat?"

"Of course, no different than the ones you would buy at the finest chocolate shop in Switzerland."

Sephie sat down next to Emmy. "We have some questions we wanted to ask you."

"The game is afoot, is it?"

"We're trying to solve a really confusing mystery."

"Excellent. What extraordinary clues have you found so far?"

Sephie had a strange feeling that Wikerus already knew what extraordinary clues they had found. "We were wondering how long Fortisians usually live."

"An intriguing question. Much depends on where they live. It they are on Fortisia, they may live as long as four centuries. If they are on a different planet, away from the Glow, they may only live half of that."

Emmy said, "What's the Glow?"

"The Glow is native to Fortisia, found nowhere else in the universe that we are aware of. It is a hybrid of sorts, both a physical life form and pure life force. It is dust floating in the air, but when touched, it transforms into the universal life force. It is everywhere on Fortisia, and is the cause of the remarkable evolutionary path which gave us our powers."

"You're saying if you're not around the Glow you age a lot faster?"

"Correct."

"Oh." Emmy stared silently at Wikerus.

"You wish to ask me something? I'm happy to answer any and all of your questions as best I can."

"Well, if you don't live as long, how come you're living here on Earth instead of Fortisia?"

"An excellent question. I live here because it has become my home. Would you travel to another world, leave all this behind, simply to live a few more years?"

Emmy shook her head. "Probably not."

Sephie said, "So it's possible that a Fortisian living in our time could have bought something from someone who lived over a hundred years ago?"

"The math is rudimentary, the answer yes. It is indeed very possible."

"Thanks."

"There is something you wish to show me?" His eyes were on Sephie's shopping bag.

Chapter 15

Professor Otto Liedenbrock

"We found this object in the basement of a house owned by someone who we think was a Fortisian. We know for certain his wife is, because we met her. She's living in the Shady Pines Retirement Facility."

"I see." Wikerus' expression was unreadable.

"Anyway, it's old, and we think he bought it from someone named Professor Otto Liedenbrock a long time ago."

A look of concern flickered crossed Wikerus' face. "Show me."

Wikerus frowned when Sephie pulled out the cube with the metal spike inside it. He stared at it silently.

Sephie tried to scan his brainwaves to see what he was thinking, but he had clouded them. He glanced up at her.

Sephie said, "Sorry, I was just… um… wondering what you were thinking about it."

"Of course."

"Do you know what it is?"

"What do you think it is?"

"We think it's from an ancient mythological boat that was in Odo's vision, and it has something to do with Odysseus. Odo said his vision seemed real. He was struggling in the water and an old man in a brown robe was pushing him under with a big wooden oar."

Wikerus leaned back in his chair, his eyes on the two friends. Emmy could hear a clock ticking in the hallway. Sephie glanced down at the floor. Why wasn't Wikerus saying anything? It must be something bad. Why was he worried about an old iron nail?

"This was a dream that Odo had?"

"It was more than that. He woke up in the night and saw spectral water in his room, but it got deeper and then turned real. It got really stormy and he thought he was going to drown. He saw me and Silas, and I think Emmy, standing on the shoreline yelling at him. The old guy in the brown robe pushed him under the water and he thought he was going to drown. Then he woke up in a dark empty void and heard a voice."

"What did the voice say?"

"It said, *'A gift of great joy and great sorrow; what was lost shall be found.'*"

Wikerus rubbed his chin. "I'm afraid I will need some time to think about this. It's far more complex than it appears, with many moving parts, much to contemplate." He looked at Emmy, studying her face.

"You have lost someone dear to you." It wasn't a question.

Emmy nodded, her voice a whisper. "My brother Jacob died in a car accident when I was little."

"I am sorry to hear that. I know how desperately painful that must have been for you, and still is, no doubt."

Emmy was silent.

Sephie said, "When do you want us to come back? Silas and Odo are researching Professor Liedenbrock and mythological boats that might have actually existed."

"I see." He rubbed his chin. "Come back in three days. There is no need for Silas and Odo to continue their research."

"You know who the Professor is?"

"Three days. When you return I will have more information for you."

"Thanks so much." Sephie stood up, smiling at Wikerus. "Say hello to Mrs. Preke for us. Silas said she hired him to work for Serendipity Salvage."

"Indeed she did. He is a marvelous young man."

Emmy said, "Thanks for helping us."

A look of empathy crossed his face. "It was my pleasure to meet you. I'm certain we will speak again."

The two friends waved good bye, heading down Expergo Street. Sephie said, "Isn't Wikerus an incredible person?"

Emmy scrunched up her face. "He was really nice and everything, but, to be honest, he was a little scary. It felt like he knew lots of stuff that he wasn't telling us, maybe scary stuff. It felt like he already knew about

Jacob, and maybe the crystal cube and Professor Liedenbrock."

Sephie laughed. "I know, that's what's so amazing. Odo gets a little creeped out by it sometimes, but he loves Wikerus. He's such a good person and he's helped us both so much."

"He is an amazing person. He seemed worried about the spike and Professor Liedenbrock. I hope it's not something bad."

"It will be fine. Let's not tell Odo and Silas he was worried, just that we have to go back in three days."

"Okay, I should get going, I have a bunch of homework to do. I'll see you at school tomorrow."

"See you!"

Sephie waved good bye, heading home. She peered into the shopping bag, eyeing the metal spike. Wikerus had seemed more than just worried, he had seemed scared.

* * * * * *

While Emmy and Sephie were visiting Wikerus, Odo and Silas were searching online for information about mythological boats and the mysterious Professor Otto Liedenbrock. It was Silas who made the first discovery.

"This can't be right."

Odo looked up from his heavy mythology book. "What can't be right?"

"I found Professor Otto Liedenbrock."

"Really? Who is he?"

"You mean who was he?"

"Okay, who was he?"

Silas flipped off the computer. "He's in the room."

"What?"

"Professor Otto Liedenbrock is in this room."

Odo stared at Silas. "Are you seeing his ghost? He's here? Can you talk to him?"

Silas got up, stepping over to his bookshelf, pulling out an old brown book. "He's in here."

"He's in a book? Who is he?"

Silas handed the book to Odo.

"*Voyage au Centre de la Terre*? What does that mean?"

"It's French for *Journey to the Center of the Earth.*

"Jules Verne wrote that. This is a first edition in French? How old is this?"

"It was published in 1868. Grandpa Mirus got it for me."

"Whoa, it must have been super expensive. A first edition of a Jules Verne book?"

"He got it for free, back in 1879."

"What?"

"Don't ask. Read the first page."

"I don't need to. I've read this book three or four times, I know the whole story; Professor Hardwigg discovers an old lava tube that goes to the center of the Earth and they have all kinds of cool adventures and get back safely."

"Read the first page."

Odo flipped the book open. "It's in French, I can't

read it."

"Read it anyway."

Odo scanned the first page, stopping and looking up at Silas. "The professor's name is Otto Liedenbrock; it's supposed to be Professor Hardwigg."

"They changed the Professor's name in the English translation. When Jules Verne first wrote it in French, he used the name Professor Otto Liedenbrock."

"It has to be a coincidence. How could a fictional character have a calling card?"

"Unless he wasn't a fictional character."

"You think he was a real person?"

"Maybe a friend of Jules Verne. Maybe he decided he didn't want his name in the book, so they changed it to Professor Hardwigg."

"That seems a little...."

"It's the only reference to him I could find. How many Professor Otto Liedenbrocks can there be?"

"If he was real, how do we find out more about him? Like where he got the spike?"

"Good question. I couldn't find anything else online."

"We can ask Wikerus. He's good at finding out stuff like that."

"Did you find any interesting mythological boats?"

"Too many of them. The Egyptians had one called the *Solar Barque*. The god of the sun, Ra, sailed it across the sky during the day and traveled to the Underworld at night, to the Land of the Dead, then came back in the morning. His boat was really fancy though, lots of jewels and gold."

"Sounds like a fun sightseeing trip. Anything else?"

"There's the *Argo*, a mythological Greek ship that Jason and the Argonauts sailed from Iolcos to Colchis to retrieve the Golden Fleece. It was big, though, lots of guys rowing it. All the boats I'm finding are too big. The one in my vision was small, twenty or thirty feet long at the most."

"Anything about Odysseus?"

"Homer's *Odyssey* says Odysseus sailed to the River of Ocean, and then to the Land of the Dead to see some prophet named Tiresias. He makes it back alive but their boat was big, definitely not the one I saw." Odo leaned back in his chair with a sigh. "None of this helps us much." He was absently flipping through the pages of Silas' book when he stopped abruptly. "No way!"

"What is it?"

Odo held up an illustration of an old bearded man in a brown robe standing in a wooden boat. "It's him! That's the guy I saw! That's the boat!"

Chapter 16

The Daguerreotype

The four friends were seated in the cafeteria, Sephie staring at the book in Odo's hands. "Do you know how crazy that sounds?"

Odo frowned. "I know what it sounds like, Sephie, but it's true. That's exactly who I saw. I'm certain of it."

"You saw Charon the Ferryman, the mythological guy who carries people across the River Styx to the Land of the Dead in his little wooden boat. Really? What are the odds of that, Odo Whitley?"

"That's the guy, Sephie. Charon the Ferryman, the River Styx, Land of the Dead, the ferry boat, the metal spike, Greek mythology? Did I forget to mention that Odysseus traveled to the Land of the Dead? It all fits, just like Mrs. Bailey said. Bingo!"

Sephie's jaw tightened. "Don't say bingo, it's extremely annoying."

"What's annoying is you not believing that I saw–"

Emmy interrupted their escalating discussion regarding Charon the Ferryman. "What about Professor Liedenbrock? Do you think he was a real person?"

Silas said, "He could be. His calling card is from the same time period that Jules Verne was alive."

"How do we find out for sure who he was?"

"We need to go see Wikerus and tell him everything we know. Maybe he can tell us more about Charon the Ferryman."

"And Professor Otto Liedenbrock."

After lunch, Odo and Sephie headed off to science class. Sephie put her hand on Odo's arm, saying, "I'm sorry I said you sounded crazy. I didn't mean it, I really didn't."

"That's okay, it does sound crazy. Sometimes I think I am crazy, having weird visions like that."

"I said it because I didn't want it to be true, I didn't want it to be Charon the Ferryman."

"Why?"

"Think about it, Odo Whitley. If it's true, if you were really there, it might mean we have to go to the Land of the Dead. I don't think many people come back from there."

Odo frowned. "I never thought about that. No way am I going there, I don't care what my vision was. That guy was crazy. Seriously, the Land of the Dead? I don't think so. Not happening."

"So you *don't* want to go to the Land of the Dead?"

"Very funny. We're not going."

"Let's go see Wikerus after school. He said we should wait three days, but we need to talk to him."

"Good idea. Maybe Mrs. Preke will be there. She has a lot of cool powers, maybe she can help us."

"I'll meet you at your locker after school."

When the final bell rang, Odo and Sephie headed for Wikerus' house.

Sephie knocked on the door and waited. There was no answer.

"I don't think anyone is home."

Odo spotted a brown envelope taped to the porch railing. "Do you think that could be for us?"

"They weren't expecting us until tomorrow."

"I know, but you know how Mrs. Preke is. She knows about stuff before it happens."

Sephie grabbed the envelope, pointing to the note on it. "It is for us." She opened it, pulling out a second smaller envelope.

"What is it?"

"There's writing on it, but it's really old and faded."

For my steadfast friend Jules,
with kindest regards

"Jules? Is he writing to Jules Verne?"

"Of course he is, Odo Whitley." Sephie opened the envelope, peering inside. "It's a photo." She pulled it out, holding it up for him to see.

"That's really old, an early one. I'm pretty sure it's a daguerreotype, high tech in the mid 1800s, when Jules Verne was alive."

"Who is it?"

Odo studied the image. "A guy standing in front of an ancient stone temple; it looks Mayan. He looks like an explorer, has the old fashioned pith helmet, explorer jacket, tall leather boots."

Sephie said, "Maybe he's an archeological mythologist."

"You think this is Professor Liedenbrock?"

"It could be. Why else would Wikerus give it to us?"

Odo flipped it over. "There's writing on the back."

At Chichén Itzá – a grand day!
Tomorrow we explore the cenotes.
September 20th, 1864
Many thanks, Otto L.

"It is him, it's Professor Liedenbrock in 1864 at a Mayan temple in Mexico. He must have sent this photo to Jules Verne. I think the Mayans believed cenotes were sacred gateways to the Underworld. They're sink holes that form when a cave collapses and fills with water. The photo was taken four years before Jules Verne wrote *Journey to the Center of the Earth*."

"Do you think Professor Liedenbrock was trying to find an entrance to the center of the Earth through a cenote?"

"In *Journey to the Center of the Earth* he finds the entrance in a volcano in Iceland, not in Mexico. I wonder why he was thanking Jules Verne?"

"I wish we knew where he got the metal spike."

"And why Emmy's brother was showing it to Silas."

"And why the golden pen led us to it."

"My head's going to explode."

"Should I run get a bucket and a mop, Odo Whitley?"

Odo stared at Sephie, then burst out laughing. "Good one, I'll have to write that down so I don't forget."

"I hate to say it, but there's only one person in the world who can help us, and he's in this photo." Sephie stared at the daguerreotype, the image triggering a memory. "Odo Whitley! I know what to do!"

"What?"

"Remember how you went back and visited Silas' grandpa Mirus in 1921?"

"With the old photo! I used it as a temporal waystone, shifting back to the time and place the photo was taken. There's only one problem, I can't talk to anyone in the past and they can't see me. I'm an invisible ghost."

"You could listen though; maybe you'll hear him say something, or find out where he got the spike and why he was thanking Jules Verne."

"It definitely could work." Odo slipped the envelope into his backpack. "I'll try it tonight."

"That's why Wikerus gave us the photo. He knew you'd done temporal shifting before."

"I wish he'd tell us stuff. I bet he knows what all this is about."

"He said once that he can't interfere in certain things, that it alters the time stream or something."

"It's still annoying, whatever the reason."

Odo called Silas when he got home, telling him about the daguerreotype and his plan to time shift back to 1864.

"Great idea, maybe the professor found the metal spike in that Mayan temple."

"It doesn't look like a Mayan artifact, it looks like a blacksmith made it."

"I'll do some more research on Charon, see what I can learn about him. Do you think the River Styx really exists, that it's a real river in some other world or dimension?"

"It could be, but why would you need to take a ferry somewhere after you die? It doesn't make sense since you don't have a physical body. On the other hand, it felt real when I was there."

"Hmm."

"What is it?"

"I was just wondering something."

"Wondering what?"

"I was wondering if Emmy's brother Jacob is in the Land of the Dead."

Chapter 17

The Temple

"I'm going to my room to study." Odo grabbed his backpack and headed up the stairs.

His dad called out, "Don't study so much, it's not good for you. Everyone knows that. I brought home two boxes of Golden CrunchCake Delights, take a break and try them. It's energy food, good for you. Helps your brain grow."

"I'll have some later, I have a big test tomorrow."

Odo's mom called out from the kitchen, "Don't stay up too late studying or you'll be listless and lethargic tomorrow."

"Okay, I won't." Odo stopped, turning slowly. That didn't sound like his mom, saying listless and lethargic instead of tired. "That's odd."

He darted up to his room, closed the door and lay down on his bed with the photo of Otto Liedenbrock. He took a long deep breath, then let it out slowly, his body relaxing. As he studied the photo, he visualized himself aligning the vibrations of his body to those of the photo, to those of the Mayan temple in 1864. Wikerus had told him to imagine an old fashioned radio dial, turning it slowly in his mind to the correct frequency. When his body began to turn solid, it would be time to make the dimensional shift.

"It's happening." His fingers were solid, then his hands.

Five seconds later he was standing in front of the Mayan temple at Chichén Itzá. "Whoa, this is incredible!"

Professor Liedenbrock was standing in front of the temple, a second man standing behind a big camera on a heavy wooden tripod, a black cloth draped over his head.

"Don't move, Professor. Rest your arm on the stone block, that will help. Stand absolutely motionless for one minute or the image will be blurred. Are you ready?"

The professor leaned against the temple wall. "Ready!"

"And, now!" There was a loud click as he opened the camera shutter. "Don't move for sixty seconds!"

Odo grinned. Technology had come a long way since 1864. It also explained why no one was ever smiling in old photos. No one could hold a smile for that long.

"Done!" He clicked the shutter again, closing it. "Excellent."

"Wonderful. I would like two prints, if you wouldn't mind. I'll send one to Jules. It was his suggestion that I explore the cenotes. The Mayans believe they are portals to the Underworld, possibly leading to the center of the Earth."

"They are filled with water, which is somewhat problematic, sir."

"We shall see, my friend, we shall see. Perhaps there is one which is not filled with water, one which shall lead to the center of the Earth."

Odo strolled across the thick spiky grass, studying the towering stone temple, imagining the time and effort it must have taken to build it. "Amazing. It's so beautiful. I wish Sephie could see this."

He followed the professor into a large white canvas tent holding three wooden cots, numerous wooden crates, and a long table covered with artifacts. Odo studied the artifacts closely. They looked Mayan, mostly stone and jade carvings, numerous beads and a few small gold figures used as pendants on stone necklaces.

"Interesting. No sign of the metal spike, though. It's definitely not a Mayan artifact. I wish I knew where it was from."

He watched Professor Liedenbrock unlock a large wooden trunk, then carefully wrap two gold figurines, putting them into a small wooden box. He gently placed the box in the massive steamer trunk. Odo stepped over to it, eyeing an eight-inch long ebony box tucked in one corner, a white label affixed to it, three words written in blue ink on the label. He froze when he read them.

Spike of Odysseus

The professor closed the trunk, locking it with a heavy brass key, exiting the tent. He called out, "Alexander, if you would please assemble the porters? I hope to arrive at the first cenote before nightfall."

Odo's mind was spinning. The ebony box was the right size for the metal spike, but why was it labeled *Spike of Odysseus*? The spike must be directly connected to him, but how? And where did the professor get it? And what did it have to do with Charon the Ferryman? Was it really from his boat? Whatever the answer was, Odo knew he wouldn't find it here. It was time to head home. He reached under his shirt for his homestone.

He closed his eyes, aligning his vibrations with the homestone. Twenty seconds later he was back on his bed, staring at the old daguerreotype.

He knew now that Professor Otto Liedenbrock was a real person, and more than likely the one who sold the metal spike to George Bailey. But where had he found it, and how was it connected to Odysseus?

At lunch the next day Odo told the others about his trip back to 1864 and what he had seen.

Emmy was stunned, whispering, "You really went back in time and saw Professor Liedenbrock at a Mayan temple?"

Odo grinned. "Just another day in the life of the incredible Translucent Boy."

"Focus, Odo Whitley. Time is money."

"If time is money, wouldn't super old people all be

really rich?"

Silas laughed. "That must be why ghosts all have such–" He stopped abruptly. "Ghosts! That's it, that's the answer!"

The other stared at him. "The answer to what?"

"To all our questions about the spike."

Odo raised his hand. "Does anyone else think Silas has gone wonky bonkers?"

"Quiet, Odo. Silas, what did you mean?"

"Odo went back and visited the professor, but he couldn't talk to him. Suppose we *could* talk to him?"

"How?"

"We talk to his ghost."

Odo gave a dark frown, shaking his head. "We're not summoning ghosts, if that's what you're thinking. Not going to happen. That's way too creepy."

Emmy nodded, "It does sound a little scary. I saw this movie where kids tried to summon a ghost and–"

"It's not scary. My grandpa has done it a bunch of times. There are a few rules though."

Odo said, "What kind of rules? We have to wear black robes and chant while we march around with flaming torches?"

Silas laughed. "No, nothing like that. We have to have a good reason to summon a ghost. It can't be for personal gain or revenge, or anything like that. It only works if you're helping someone."

"Who are we helping?"

Silas glanced at Emmy. "I think we're helping Emmy, but I don't exactly know how."

Sephie shrugged. "Let's try it, Odo Whitley. The worst that can happen is you'll get carried off to Hades by a giant hairy demon."

"Why did you say that? Did you have a vision?"

Emmy snickered. Sephie could be so funny sometimes.

Chapter 18

The Professor's Tale

The four friends sat facing each other in Silas' living room.

Silas looked at them, his expression solemn. "Okay, everyone put on your black robe, light your torch, and start chanting."

Sephie burst out laughing.

Odo rolled his eyes. "Ha ha. Just to be clear, I wasn't being serious when I said that."

"Sorry, I couldn't help it. Okay, my grandpa told me what to do. It's pretty simple, I just ask for the ghost's help, ask him to be here. They don't travel like we do, they can just be wherever they want. The Professor will know if our reasons are self-serving. If they are, he won't show up. You won't be able to see him, but I will. If he shows up, which he may not, I'll tell you everything he–" Silas stopped, staring across the room.

"What is it?"

"Uhh... he's here?"

"No way."

"Way."

"Ask him where he got the metal spike?"

Odo blinked when the blue shimmering figure appeared, a voice sounding in his mind.

"You may ask me yourself, Odo Whitley."

Odo looked at the others. "Did you hear that? Do you see him?"

They all nodded, their eyes on the flickering blue spectral image of Professor Otto Liedenbrock.

"I've never talked to a ghost before."

"Yes, yes, what is your question? Time is money." The professor threw his head back, giving a raucous laugh. He winked at Sephie.

"You sold the black metal spike to George Bailey?"

"The Spike of Odysseus. Yes, quite true, I sold it to him in 1907 in New York City."

"Where did you get it? What is it, exactly?"

"I was on an archeological dig in Greece, on the island of Ithaca, to be more precise. I had believed for quite some time that Odysseus was more than a mythological being, that he had been a real person. We were searching for his tomb."

"Why?"

"To prove he existed. There was a tale that he had been accidentally killed on the island of Ithaca by his own son, Telegonus, who had mistaken him for someone else. We tried unsuccessfully for several months to find the tomb, until one day we passed a large rock, faintly visible ancient Greek letters on it, written from right to

111

left as would be expected. We were able to make out the last five letters of Odysseus' name.

That was enough for us, so we began digging. Two days later we had uncovered a sword, some armor, and half a dozen clay amphorae, but no burial tomb. Inside one of the amphorae was a crudely formed black metal spike wrapped in a sheepskin scroll. The scroll claimed that Odysseus had brought the spike back from the Land of the Dead."

"Are you serious?"

"*Quite serious, indeed, young man. There is more to this tale. The scroll also claimed that Odysseus had pulled the spike out of Charon's ferry, furious that he would force souls to pay for their passage across the River Styx to the Land of the Dead. The spike he took was the Key Spike, without which, Charon's ferry could not operate properly.*"

"Do you think it's true?"

The professor smiled, a smile that Odo had seen on Wikerus Praevian when he knew a lot more than he was saying. "*One never knows about such things. Perhaps you are destined to find a deeper truth which lies beyond the spike.*"

"What are we supposed to do with the spike?"

"*If you found a wallet filled with gold coins on the street, what would you do?*"

"Try to find out who dropped it and return it to them?"

Professor Liedenbrock gave the curious smile again. "*There is one more thing which may be of some certain*

112

interest to you."

Odo was suddenly suspicious. "What one thing?"

"The scroll said that Charon is offering a reward for the return of the Key Spike."

"What kind of reward?"

"Whoever returns it will be allowed to bring one person back from the Land of the Dead."

Emmy put her hand over her mouth. "I could bring Jacob back. I could bring him back."

The professor smiled. *"Of course there is no real proof that the contents of the scroll bear any resemblance to reality, that the spike truly was taken from Charon's ferry, or that he is indeed offering such a reward."*

Emmy said, "If we did want to return it, how would we do it? How do we get there?"

"An excellent question indeed, young lady, and I wish you the very best of luck in discovering the answer." With a wave of his hand, Professor Otto Liedenbrock faded to nothingness.

The four friends stared at each other, stunned by the Professor's revelations.

Odo was the first to speak. "Okay, that's it. Game over. No way are we going to the Land of the Dead. Anyone hungry? I could make some cookies. Silas, do you have any ice cream?"

Sephie didn't have to read Odo's brainwaves to know he was terrified.

"Odo Whitley, you need to think. We don't have to go to the Land of the Dead. Charon's ferry goes from the Land of the Living across the River Styx to the Land of the Dead. We could give him the Key Spike on the Land of the Living side of the River Styx."

Odo was silent for moment, then said, "That makes sense. We don't actually have to visit the Land of the Dead, do we?" His smile reappeared. "Did you say you had ice cream?" He stepped into the kitchen.

Emmy said, "Do you think it's really possible to bring someone back from the Land of the Dead? What is the Land of the Dead, exactly?"

"Odo and I went to a place called Palusia, where people who died create their own worlds, but they were more like dream worlds. The Land of the Dead sounds different, but we really have no idea what it's like."

"Do you think we should try to return the Key Spike to Charon the Ferryman?"

"It sounded like Professor Liedenbrock thought that would be the right thing to do. Everything that's happened has been pointing us in that direction."

"If we did bring Jacob back, would he be older than... when he left?"

"I don't know."

Silas said, "This is all unknown territory, we really need to talk to Wikerus about it. We shouldn't do anything until we find out more about where we're going. Odo said we can use the Key Spike as a waystone, but we have no idea where it was made, if it was even the same world that Charon lives in. We also don't know what Charon's world is like. The ancient Greeks had stories about him, but who knows how reliable they are."

"Or if time is the same there. There are places where time acts a lot differently than it does here. Some places don't even have time."

Emmy gave a long sigh. "I don't want anyone to get hurt."

Odo called out, "Can I have some of these cookies?"

Chapter 19

Nomi

Emmy pulled the covers over her, her thoughts confused, conflicted. She wanted to bring Jacob back, but she didn't want anything to happen to Sephie or Odo, and especially not to Silas. These were her first true friends, friends who didn't notice her crooked legs, friends who saw who she really was. She had told them about the Cube and they still liked her. She had never had that before. It was nice not to have dark secrets hiding inside her.

She closed her eyes, visualizing the Cube. Maybe she could find some answers there. Maybe Nomi could tell her what to do, guide her.

She woke up inside the Cube, stepping over to the key pad, entering the passcode. She whispered, "Nomi, I need your help. I don't know what to do."

She was stunned by the beauty of the world she saw when the door slid open; vast rolling meadows filled with great swaths of brilliant wildflowers, magnificent towering shade trees, a sparkling lake, colorful birds soaring across the sky.

She breathed in the sweet fragrance of the green grass and flowers. "This is so amazing. Maybe this is what the Land of the Dead is like." She blinked when she saw a shining castle appear on a distant meadow. "It's so beautiful. I wonder who lives there?"

She raised her arms, floating up into the air, soaring toward the castle, circling around it. It was stunning, like something out of a fairy tale. She wished she could live there. She wished Silas and Odo and Sephie could live there with her. She landed softly in front of the main gate, a voice calling down from the watchtower.

"Who goes there? What is the purpose of your visit?"

"I'm Emmeline Snow and I'm trying to find Nomi, my dream guide. I need her help."

"I see. What kind of help?"

"I don't know what to do. I can bring my brother back from the Land of the Dead, but I don't want anything to happen to my friends. I've never had friends like them before."

"One moment please. I will inform Nomi of your wishes."

"She's here? I can see her?"

Emmy took a step back when the castle gates silently swung open. She stared at the young girl who stepped out, a young girl with crooked legs.

Emmy said, "You're me. I don't understand. Why am I seeing myself?"

"I'm Nomi, your guide."

"But you look like me."

"That is because I am you."

"I'm confused."

"You are able to fly in this world?"

Emmy nodded. "I flew here from the Cube. Your castle is amazing."

"You mean your castle. You flew here? Curious, since this is a real world, not a dream world."

"What? It's real?"

"Show me. Fly for me. Prove yourself, Emmeline Snow."

"But… okay." Emmy raised her arms. Nothing happened. "I can't fly in real worlds." She noticed her legs were crooked now, just like Nomi's.

"And yet you flew here from the Cube. Can you explain that?"

"I thought it was a dream world."

"And what happened when I told you the world was real?"

"I could feel the weight of the world, the gravity pulling me down, my real body returning, my legs twisted again."

"Where did the change occur?"

"What do you mean?"

"When you arrived here you could fly, but after you heard my words, you could not. Where did the change occur?"

"In my head? When you said the world was real, I knew I couldn't fly."

118

"Exactly. Your own mind decided you should use a physical body, not a dream body. You are the one who decides whether or not you can fly. Do you understand?"

Emmy nodded. "I think so, but I don't really understand who you are. How can you be me when I'm right here?"

Nomi stepped over to Emmy, taking her hands. "I am a physical manifestation of a deeper, hidden part of you, your inner self. You were not aware of me in the past, but now you are. It is time for you to make a choice, to decide whether or not to merge your consciousness with mine, your inner self. If you do so, you will no longer need me as a guide. You will be your own guide. Be aware that your life will be forever changed. You will see the world far differently, becoming aware of the infinite hidden connections which lie beneath all things, the secret threads that are woven together to form the grand tapestry of life."

"That sounds a little scary, merging myself with another consciousness. What do you think I should do?"

"You are the one who must decide, not me."

Emmy said, "I've learned so much from you, and I do trust you. You're really a deeper part of me that has always been there?"

"I am."

"I'll do it, I'll merge with you. Does it take long to–"

There was a flash of white light, Nomi's form vanishing.

"Is that it? Did you do it?" Fear shot through Emmy. What exactly had she done?

A thought popped into her head. All transitions were chaotic, often scary, especially discovering your deeper self, the self within, realizing you are far more than you thought you were, that the universe is far different than you thought it was. She remembered Sephie saying something about her deeper self, but she hadn't paid much attention to it.

"Nomi?"

There was no answer, but she knew Nomi was there, that she and Nomi were the same person now. "Is this a real world, or is it a dream world?"

Another thought popped into her head. It didn't matter if it was a dream or if it was real, she had the power to transform her body into a dream body wherever she was.

She held out her arms, floating up into a clear blue sky, gazing down at the rolling hills and meadows.

"I can fly."

She landed in a glorious meadow filled with bright yellow wildflowers and lay down, breathing in the delicate fragrance of the flowers, running one hand through the soft grass.

"What should I do about Jacob? Should I bring him back from the Land of the Dead? I want to, but I–"

She knew the answer before she had finished asking the question. All transitions were chaotic, scary, and difficult. This one would be no different. She also knew that chaos always leads to order.

It was time to bring Jacob home.

When she woke up in her bed she saw two glowing words floating in front of her.

Know me.

She laughed. "Nomi."

Chapter 20

Arcadia

Silas studied Emmy's face, searching for any sign of doubt. "You're sure you want to do it?"

"I'm sure, I want to bring Jacob back. I know it could be dangerous, but we'll be okay." She hadn't told them about her visit with Nomi, or what had happened.

Silas turned to Odo and Sephie. "What do you think?"

Odo grinned. "I think Emmy needs a superhero name."

Emmy shook her head. "Not yet, maybe when we get back."

"Wikerus said it was okay to use the Key Spike as a waystone?"

"He said it's the only way to get there."

"Did he say where it will take us?"

"Of course not. He did say it would be very interesting though."

Silas frowned. "What does that mean?"

"It means it will be very interesting."

"Like we'll get eaten by very interesting monsters?"

"I don't think that's what he meant. He wouldn't send us to a place like that."

Emmy said, "How long do you think we'll be there? If I'm gone too long my mom will get worried."

"Not a problem. Even if we spend a month there, when we come back only an hour will have passed here."

"How is that possible?"

Odo said, "Time flows at different rates in different worlds, but with dimensional shifting, when we come back to this world only one hour will have passed. Wikerus tried to explain it to me, but it was a little confusing, especially the math, which was ridiculously complicated. Actually, when I think about it, I guess I have no idea at all how it works, just that it does."

"Did he say what would happen if we bring Jacob back?"

Odo glanced at Sephie.

"He wasn't sure. He said there's no way of knowing how it will change your life, that events like this are unpredictable, often with unforeseen consequences."

Emmy was silent for a moment. "Do you think I might die in the accident instead of Jacob? That he might come back, but I won't, that I would be trading my life for his? That you never would have known me?"

Silas shook his head. "Not a chance. That's not going to happen."

Sephie did not look as convinced, but said nothing.

Odo said, "We're superheroes, we'll be fine."

Emmy said, "You're right. You have the Key Spike?"

"Wikerus let me pull it out of the crystal cube. It tingles a little but it's not as powerful as I thought it was. We're good to go." He turned to Sephie, raising one eyebrow. "Let's rock and roll."

Sephie grinned, striking a classic superhero pose. "It's showtime!"

Emmy raised one fist in the air, her other hand on her hip. "Let's do this!"

Silas stared at them. "Really? You're all doing that? Seriously?"

Odo pulled the black spike from his pack. "Okay, everyone hold hands and I'll shift us there. You might feel a little disoriented, maybe nauseous, when we arrive."

"You better not barf on me, Odo."

Odo snorted, aligning his vibrations with the deep vibrations of the Key Spike, imagining the old fashioned radio dial turning to the correct frequency.

"Your hands are solid!"

"Here we go!"

A split second later their world vanished, replaced by a bucolic farmland scene, a dozen sheep milling about behind a rustic wooden split rail fence. Odo turned at the sound of hammering, spotting a burly blacksmith pounding a strip of red hot metal with a heavy iron hammer. Past the blacksmith shop lay a small town pulled from a picture book, brightly painted wooden houses, hard packed dirt streets, a few people riding horses.

Emmy was staring at Odo. "I can see you. You're solid."

Odo nodded. "I'm only translucent on Earth. I'm solid on other worlds."

Emmy leaned over, whispering something to Sephie. They both looked at Odo and grinned, Sephie nodding.

Odo frowned. "What are you laughing about?"

"Secret girl stuff, Odo Whitley. Nothing you'd be interested in."

"Right."

Silas said, "This is not at all what I was expecting."

Odo pointed to the blacksmith. "I told you the spike was made by an old fashioned blacksmith."

"You do realize the River Styx might not be in this world, right?"

"Let's find out, Encephalo Girl." Odo strolled over to the blacksmith shop.

The bearded blacksmith put his hammer down, wiping his hands on a leather apron. "How can I help you folks?"

Odo held up the Key Spike. "Did you make this?"

The blacksmith studied it, then nodded. "That one and ten thousands others just like it."

"What is this place?"

"Welcome to Arcadia, friend."

"Are we near the Land of the Dead?"

The blacksmith gazed at the four friends. "You're all

dead?"

"No, we're not dead, not even a little bit. We're trying to find Charon the Ferryman on the River Styx."

"I thought you said you weren't dead?"

"We're not, but we have some business with him."

"What kind of business would you have with someone like that?"

Odo answered the question with another question. "Did you build Charon's boat?"

"I don't build boats; I'm a blacksmith, not a boatwright."

"Do you know who built it? I think this spike came from his boat."

"I sell a lot of ship spikes to The Enchanted Boatworks in South Elysium. They're on the banks of the Summerland River. Most likely they built his boat."

"How far is that from here?"

"It's a two day walk, down that road. Lovely scenery, beautiful weather. South Elysium is a charming community." He grinned.

"Why are you grinning?"

"It's an odd place. Quirky. Not like Arcadia. You'll see."

"Quirky like what?"

"Quirky like quirky. I have to get back to work." The blacksmith turned, heading back to his shop.

Odo frowned, adjusting his backpack. "I guess we walk there. Unless someone wants to carry me?"

Silas laughed. "He was right about the nice weather. Should be a fun walk."

"Maybe we'll find a nice place to stop for lunch."

Sephie said, "I brought a box of granola bars just in case."

As they headed off down the road, Emmy said, "I need to tell you guys something. It's about Nomi, my dream guide. Something happened."

Chapter 21

South Elysium

"You flew in a real world, not a dream world?"

"I think so, but it's confusing. Nomi said I could decide which body I had, a dream body or a real one."

"That doesn't seem possible; how could you change your physical body into a dream body?"

"You do it every night in your dreams. You create a dream body so you can interact in the dream world. Your physical body is sleeping in your bed."

"That's true, but how is it possible? How do you do it?"

"I don't know, but I could fly in Nomi's world and she said it was a real world."

"Maybe it wasn't real, maybe she just said that. Can you fly here?"

"I don't want to try."

"Why?"

"I just don't."

Silas said, "It's okay, whatever the reason is."

"I'm scared I won't be able to fly, and then I'll know."

Silas studied her face. "Know what?"

"I'll know I'm not special, that I can't fly, that I'm just Emmeline, the crazy girl who hides in the Cube because she's afraid of life."

"Why would you hide in the Cube when you have three fantastic friends like us who really like you and want you with us when we visit weird alien worlds?"

Emmy smiled. "Thanks, Silas. That's so nice to hear."

Sephie called out, "Does anyone want a granola bar?"

Odo rubbed his stomach. "That's weird, we've been walking for hours and I'm not hungry. Or tired."

"Neither am I, Odo Whitley. That's very peculiar, especially for you. You're always hungry."

Silas said, "I'm not hungry either. Or thirsty."

"Let's try running, see if we get tired."

"Let's just enjoy the walk, Odo Whitley. It doesn't always have to be a race."

"It's not a race, Sephie, I just want to understand what's happening, how this world works." He turned to Silas. "Race you to the Enchanted Boatworks?"

"You're on." Silas skittered backwards, a terrified expression on his face. He pointed to something behind Odo. "FIRE BREATHING DRAGON!"

Odo spun around, his eyes on the rippling green sky. "Where?" He whipped back around when he heard Silas racing down the dirt road laughing.

"Cheater!" Odo took off after him, his legs a blur. "Whoa! This is crazy! No way should I be running this fast."

Two minutes later he caught up to Silas. "How fast are we going?"

"Really fast! Maybe thirty miles an hour. Are your legs tired?"

"Not at all, I'm not even out of breath."

"This is so cool, I wish I could run like this back home. I'd win a million medals and be in the Olympics."

"Do you think Emmy can really fly, or was that whole thing with Nomi just a dream?"

"The part about her deeper self sounded real. Wikerus has told me a lot about it. He said it knows a lot more than our conscious self knows and I should try to listen to what it tells me. He said our dreams are like postcards from our deeper self, but it can be hard to understand what they mean."

"If she could fly in the real world, people might say she was a witch or a demon, or even an angel. That wouldn't be good. She couldn't have a normal life."

"That's true. She could fly around at night though. That would be fun. Except it would be dark. And kind of scary."

"Up ahead, it looks like a town!"

"Check out the sign!"

The two friends slid to a stop, sending up a cloud of dust. Silas eyed the large green and white sign.

Welcome to South Elysium

Seconds later there was a blur of motion, Sephie and Emmy screeching to a halt in front of them. Emmy ran ahead and touched the sign, a huge grin on her face. "I win! How fun was that?"

Silas laughed, then stopped, his eyes on Emmy's legs. He pointed to them. "Um… your legs… they…"

"They're straight. That happens in dream worlds."

Odo said, "But this isn't a dream world. We shifted here in our physical bodies, and we're not sleeping, not dreaming that we're here."

Emmy shrugged. "I don't want to think about it. I'm having fun. It doesn't matter if it's real or a dream. We should just enjoy it."

Sephie nodded her agreement. "You don't need to understand everything, Odo Whitley. Some things are just meant to be enjoyed."

"You're right. It was so much fun to run like that."

The four friends strolled past the sign, Odo pointing to the village ahead of them. "It looks like an old English village, like a fairy tale."

Two laughing children dressed in old fashioned clothes darted out from behind a tree, stopping when they saw the four strangers. "Who are you?"

Sephie gave them a bright smile. "My name is Sephie. We came to see your beautiful town. It's so lovely."

"It's called South Elysium. Mama says it's the best

131

town there is."

"Wow, it must be really nice."

Odo said, "We're trying to find the Enchanted Boatworks. Do you know where that is?"

"Everyone knows where it is, it's where they make all the boats. How come you don't know where it is?"

"We've never been here before. Can you show us how to get there?"

"Okay, follow us!"

They strolled along behind the children, Odo's eyes on the cozy cottages with thatched roofs that lined the road. "Check out their gardens."

"So many different kinds of roses. They're beautiful."

A woman wearing a long pale green dress pushed open her front gate, stepping out to greet them. "Hello, friends. Isn't it a lovely day?"

"It is beautiful. I love your garden, the flowers are stunning."

"How kind of you to say so. Are you from Arcadia?"

"No, we're from far away. We came here to visit the Enchanted Boatworks, to ask them about a boat they made."

"How lovely. You'll find them about a mile from here on the banks of the Summerland River."

"Our new friends here are showing us the way."

The two children giggled. "They don't know where anything is!"

"That's because they don't live here, they're from far away, and you know what that means."

"We have to be extra nice to them because everyone is a precious gift, even people we don't know."

"Exactly right." The woman turned with a wave. "Have a lovely day, enjoy your walk and this beautiful weather."

"Thank you so much for your help."

Odo glanced over to Silas. "Everyone here seems really nice. Really, really, really nice."

"I know. It's a little odd."

"Maybe that's what the blacksmith meant about them being quirky."

"Probably. Oh well, at least they're not carnivorous aliens trying to eat us."

"True."

It took almost an hour to reach the Enchanted Boatworks, dozens of villagers stopping to talk with them, each one friendlier and chattier than the one before.

Odo whispered, "This is making me crazy."

Sephie said, "It is a little odd. I'm getting a strange feeling."

"What kind of strange feeling?"

"I don't know yet."

Emmy spotted sparkling blue water through the trees. "It's the Summerland River!"

Chapter 22

The Enchanted Boatworks

The two children ran ahead, pointing to a long low wooden structure surrounded by wooden boats in various stages of construction. One of them turned around, calling out, "Here it is, people from far away! This is the Enchanted Boatworks! Bye! Have a wonderful day!"

"Thank you so much for helping us!"

Odo whispered. "You don't have to say thank you to everyone."

"I'm just being polite, Odo Whitley."

Odo gave her a ridiculously pleasant smile. "I apologize, friend, and thank you ever so much for being so polite. It's such a lovely day and you've made it even lovelier just because of the way you–"

"I'm going to vaporize you, Odo Whitley!"

Odo grinned, stepping over to one of the boats, a

man in worn coveralls using an old fashioned hand plane to smooth one of the ship's beams. He waved to the man. "Good afternoon."

"And a good afternoon to you, sir. How may I help you?"

"We wanted to talk to someone about a boat you may have made. We have a ship spike that we think came from the boat." Odo pulled out the spike, handing it to the man.

He studied the spike. "Excellent, this is all I need. Follow me, if you would."

They trailed behind the man into the long building, Odo spotting half a dozen more boats in the final stages of construction.

Silas eyed the lustrous wooden crafts. "Wow, those are beautiful, amazing craftsmanship."

"Thank you so much, how kind of you to say so. Here we are."

Odo stopped short when he saw a gleaming silver and glass machine covered with tiny blinking lights, the device emitting a low humming sound. This was definitely a very high tech machine. He had no idea what it did. "What is that?"

"As a courtesy to our customers, each piece of the boat receives a unique twenty digit code at the base quantum level. If a part breaks, we scan it for the identifying code and replace the part at no charge. All our boats have a lifetime workmanship guarantee."

"Right, quantum level code. Clever." Odo looked at Silas, his eyebrows raised.

The man pulled a glowing blue orb from a rack on the device, holding it next to the metal spike. He frowned, tapping the orb. "This is a Key Spike. Where did you say you got it?"

"Um, we just found it somewhere and someone said you might have used it in a boat you made?"

"Of course, indeed, very good." The man cleared his throat. "There doesn't appear to be any defects in the spike, so we won't be able to replace it. Unfortunately, even if it were damaged, we would not be able to replace a Key Spike. We don't make those here."

"I don't want to replace it, just return it to the original owner."

"I see, how very thoughtful of you. Very good, indeed. One moment please, if you wouldn't mind. I just have to check with my superior." The man stepped into an office, closing the door behind him. Several minutes later he stepped out again.

"I do hate to be a bother, but might I inquire as to your current state of being?"

"What do you mean?"

"There really is no delicate way to ask this, I'm afraid. Are you dead?"

"We're not dead. Why does everyone keep asking us that?"

"I do apologize, it's a mere formality of course, nothing personal, I assure you. Rules are rules, as you well know. If you were dead, I would be obliged to confiscate the Key Spike. Since you are quite alive, the spike is yours to do with as you see fit. I don't know if you are familiar with the original owner, but his chosen name is Charon the Ferryman. His business is located on the River Styx, three hundred miles south of here."

"He's the one who ferries people to the Land of the Dead, right?"

"Indeed, quite so. He only ferries dead people, of course, in the odd chance you were contemplating a sightseeing venture into the Land of the Dead."

"Definitely not planning that. Not going to happen." Odo took the Key Spike from the man. "We just head south?"

"Follow the Summerland River south for three hundred and nine miles until it merges into the River Styx. Travel east at the confluence for fifteen miles and you'll find Charon's Crossing."

"Thanks for all your help."

"Of course, of course, you are more than welcome."

The four friends headed down the dirt road toward the town center.

"Did you see that weird machine? How did they get crazy high tech stuff like that when all they have is wooden boats and hand tools?"

Silas shook his head. "It's definitely strange. Something odd is going on here."

"Do you see any ghosts?"

"Now that you mention it, I haven't seen any. That's odd."

The two young girls reappeared, skipping toward them, stopping. "Did you find the Enchanted Boatworks, people from far away?"

"We did, thank you so much. Now we're on our way to the River Styx to meet someone."

"Don't forget to wake the Sleeper." The two girls looked at each other, one of them covering her mouth, both of them giggling.

Emmy kneeled down in front of them. "You both seem so nice. Who is the Sleeper?"

The girl whispered, "It's a secret. We aren't supposed to tell anyone or go near him. We shouldn't have told you."

"I was just curious about who he is. I know, why don't you tell me what you want to be when you grow up?"

"When we what?"

"Grow up, like your mom."

The girls looked at each other, scrunching up their faces.

"Like my mom?"

"Yes, when you're big like your mom. What will you do?"

The girls burst out laughing. "Why would we be big like our mom? We're kids. You're silly! Is everyone from far away silly like you?"

Sephie studied the two children. "How old are you?"

"Are you being silly again?"

"Maybe just a little. How long have you lived here?"

"We've always lived here." The girls ran off laughing.

Odo said, "They don't know how old they are?"

"I noticed something curious about their brainwaves.

They didn't understand what it means to grow up."

"Are you saying people here don't grow old? They just stay the way they are?"

"It's starting to look like that."

"This place is officially giving me the creeps."

"What's that building over there?" Silas pointed through the trees to a gleaming silver structure.

"That looks out of place. Let's go check it out."

They stepped through the dense foliage, emerging in front of a twenty-foot wide silver dome.

"Not exactly rustic looking."

"There's a keypad next to the door. More high tech stuff."

"How do we get in?"

Odo stepped over to the structure, placing his hand on the outer wall, a shimmering translucent doorway appearing. "Let's check it out." He followed the others in, stopping short when he saw the large red button on the wall. Beneath the button was a three-foot wide red sign with bold white letters.

DO NOT
UNDER ANY CIRCUMSTANCES
PUSH THE RED BUTTON!
–The South Elysium Department
Of Maintenance and Operations

Chapter 23

Odo's Dilemma

Odo stared at the shiny fire engine red button. "What do you think it is?"

"A big red button that we're not supposed to push."

"Right, but why would they have a button if you're not supposed to push it?"

"Because it might do something dangerous?"

"I get that, but the dome is securely locked, so the villagers can't get in. If they can't get in, why bother with a big sign saying don't push the button?"

"I know what you're thinking, Odo Whitley, and you need to stop thinking it. You're not going to push the button just to see what it does."

"I don't want to push it, I just want to know what it does. They shouldn't have put that sign on it. Why would they do that?"

"We should leave. It could be something really dangerous, maybe something that vaporizes us, or sprays out a deadly toxin, or opens a door and horrible poisonous spiders come streaming out."

Odo shook his head. "If that was true, the sign would

warn us. It would say, 'Danger! If you push the red button you'll be instantly vaporized, poisoned, and bitten by swarms of deadly spiders.'" He inched closer to the button. "Don't forget, it could do something super cool, like open the door to a secret vault filled with gold coins."

"If that was true they would tell you to push it, not to not push it."

"We have to push it, Sephie. We have to!"

"Odo Whitley, do not touch that–"

Odo slapped the button.

The four friends froze.

Nothing happened.

Nothing happened again.

And again.

"I don't get it. What does it do?"

"Maybe it was a test, a test you failed miserably, Odo Whitley."

"Or I passed with flying colors for thinking outside the box."

Sephie shook her head, mumbling something.

"What did you say?"

"Nothing. Let's go."

They exited the dome, heading back through the trees to the town center.

Silas stopped short. "Whoa."

"No one is moving. They all look like statues."

Emmy ran over to a man wearing a dark brown tweed suit. "He's not breathing." She poked his shoulder, but the man didn't move.

"They're all like that. Look at the kids playing, they're frozen."

"I guess we know what the red button does, Odo Whitley."

"You can't turn people off with a button, Sephie."

Silas said, "Unless they're not people."

"They're machines?"

"Technically they'd be androids."

"We're in a town filled with androids? That makes no sense at all. Who put the red button there, and why? And who gave them the crazy high tech machine at the Enchanted Boatworks?"

Emmy said, "Let's check out the town. We can look in their houses. If they are androids, they won't have food or water."

"They probably drink motor oil and eat ground up metal."

Silas snorted. "Good one."

Emmy ran over to a window, peering into one of the cottages. "There's an old man sitting in a chair looking at a photograph. He's frozen, but he has a sad look on his face. It's the first one I've seen who doesn't look happy."

Odo ran over to a cottage, opening the front door. He peeked in, then stepped inside. "No kitchen, no sink, no bathroom. They're definitely androids."

"What do we do? Should we push the red button again? Do you think that would start them up?"

"I'll try it." Odo ran back to the dome, pushing the red button. When he returned the androids were still frozen.

Sephie glared at him. "I told you not to push that button, Odo Whitley."

"It's a big red button, how could I not push it?"

Emmy said, "I bet whoever put the button there will come back and restart the town. The androids won't starve or anything. They'll start moving again and not even know they stopped."

"Odo said, "I have an idea."

"That never ends well."

"What? It's a fantastic idea. Instead of walking three hundred miles to Charon's Crossing, we can take a nice leisurely boat ride down the Summerland River."

Sephie said, "That's actually not a bad idea. It would be fun to drift down the river, relaxing."

"Is anyone hungry yet? Or thirsty?"

"Not me."

"Or me."

"Let's go see if we can find a boat."

They headed through the town, peering into some of the shops along the way.

"It's all old fashioned stuff, like people had before there was electricity. Androids should all have super high tech machines and flying vehicles."

Sephie said. "Unless they don't know they're androids."

Odo turned to Silas. "I just had an interesting thought. What if the androids don't know they're androids?"

"I just said that, Odo Whitley."

Odo slapped his leg, laughing.

Emmy said, "I bet you're right, Sephie. I bet they don't know they're machines."

"It's interesting, but it's not why we're here. Let's go find a boat." Odo wanted to put the red button incident behind him.

"We go that way."

Odo pointed to the docks. "It's showtime."

"It's not even close to showtime, Odo Whitley. We're taking a leisurely cruise down the Summerland River in a lovely hand crafted wooden boat. There's nothing showtime about it."

Chapter 24

The Wall

"This is perfect, the sign says the boats are for public use. We just have to return it when we're done."

"Let's take that one, it has plenty of room, padded seats and two sets of oars."

Sephie gave Odo a questioning look. "Do you even know how to row a boat, Odo Whitley?"

"Are you forgetting we were kidnapped by pirates on Plindor and I had to row on the galley ship Canthus? I am an expert at rowing, undoubtedly the best rower here."

"How silly of me, I must have forgotten about the Canthus. Since you're such an expert, you can do all the rowing." Sephie gave Odo a sweet smile.

Odo frowned. "You tricked me."

Silas hopped into the boat, grabbing two oars. "Don't forget, we don't get tired here."

"Oh, right." Odo took a seat behind Silas.

Emmy and Sephie jumped in, Emmy untying the boat and pushing them off.

Sephie leaned back in her seat. "What a beautiful

day. Get busy rowing, Odo Whitley."

"Aye aye, Captain Sephie. I'll row us out into the current and we can drift down the river."

"We could have a picnic while we're floating down-river."

"We don't need to eat or drink here."

"We could be androids and not know it."

"I'm pretty sure you're an android."

"Ha ha."

Sephie abruptly sat up. "I just remembered something."

"What?"

"That little girl said don't forget to wake the Sleep-er."

"Who's the Sleeper?"

"She said she couldn't tell us, it was a secret."

"That helps a lot." Odo looked up and down the shoreline. "I don't see anything that looks like a Sleeper."

"Maybe she was just making up a story. Kids do that."

"She's an android, they don't make things up."

The boat rounded a wide turn in the river, Silas using the oars to keep them away from the shoreline.

Odo was the first to see it. "What is that?" He point-ed to a massive wall of fog running across the river about a half mile ahead of them.

Silas studied the curious anomaly. "Is that a storm? It's weird that it looks like a big wall."

Sephie furrowed her brow. "I'm getting a bad feeling

about this. I think it has something to do with the Sleeper."

"Like what?"

"I'm not sure. I guess we just drift into it and see what happens."

"That doesn't sound like a very well thought out plan."

"Do you have a better one?"

"Not unless you have a helicopter in your back-pack."

Ten minutes later Odo yawned. "I'm tired. I need a nap."

"I'm tired too. It's weird because we're not supposed to get tired here."

Sephie leaned against the side of the boat, her eyes closing.

Emmy curled up in her seat. "So sleepy, it's nice and warm."

Odo woke up, giving a start when he saw the dock, saw the town. "What happened? How did we get back here?"

Sephie opened her eyes, stopping halfway through a yawn. "We're back at the dock. How did that happen?"

Silas said, "It wasn't me, I was sound asleep the whole time."

Emmy eyed the village. "The little girl told us we had to wake the Sleeper. Maybe this is what happens if you don't wake him, you hit the wall of fog, fall asleep, and come back to South Elysium."

"That makes sense in a crazy alien world sort of

way. How do we find the Sleeper?"

Silas let out a yelp. "Over there! I saw something blue moving through the trees. It's heading toward the silver dome."

"Let's go check it out!"

The four friends hopped out of the boat, running along the dock. Before they reached the shore, the androids started moving again.

"Whoa! Whoever you saw must have turned the androids back on."

They raced through the trees toward the dome, darting into the clearing just in time to see a man wearing grease stained blue coveralls and a ratty old San Diego Padres baseball cap step out of the silver dome. He gave a surprised look, then vanished in a blink of blue light.

"No way!"

"Way. I'd recognize him anywhere."

Silas said, "You know who that was?"

"We met him in Palusia, the place where people who have passed on create their own personal worlds of thought. His name is Mike the Mechanic."

"That's an odd name."

"You have no idea how weird that guy is. He made us take some ridiculous three question challenge, told us if we missed all three questions we'd be eaten by hungry rabid weasels."

The color drained from Emmy's face. "Rabid weasels? That's horrible. I don't like weasels. They're so scary."

"I'm not sure if he was serious or not. It's hard to tell with him."

"Either way, he's gone now. We need to find the Sleeper and wake him, whatever he is."

"I'll ask that guy over there." Odo darted across the grass to an android sweeping a stone walkway.

"Hi, my name is Odo."

"Hello, Odo. I do hope you're having a lovely day. Are you taking a boat ride today?"

"We were trying to, but we ran into a big wall of fog and woke up back here again. Do you know anything about someone called the Sleeper?"

"You picked a lovely day for a boat ride. There are some parasols in the shed if the sky is too bright for you."

"That sounds perfect, thank you so much, but, do you know who the Sleeper is and how we wake him?"

"I go for a boat ride once a week with my two grandchildren. We always have such a marvelous time."

"Uhh, thanks." Odo ran back to the others. "He won't answer any questions about the Sleeper. It's like he doesn't even hear them."

"He's probably programmed not to answer them."

"So we're on our own."

"Let's try the boat again, but this time stick close to the shore and keep our eyes open for anything odd, anything that looks like a Sleeper, whatever that is."

Silas rowed them over to the far side of the river. "Check out those wooden cabins in the trees. Looks like people live here."

"Androids?"

"I can't tell."

"There's a guy fishing downriver at the third dock. Maybe he can tell us something."

Silas rowed them toward the dock, Odo eyeing the grizzled old man sitting in a canvas folding chair. He wore a pair of round dark blue sunglasses, a floppy hat with hooks in it, and a tattered vest with a half dozen pockets. His fishing line was in the water, a red and white bobber floating a few feet from the dock.

Odo called out, "Excuse me! Could you help us?"

The old man didn't respond.

"Maybe he's deaf."

They tied the boat up, hopping onto the dock.

Sephie tapped the old man's shoulder. "Excuse me, sir, could you help us?"

"What wrong with him? He's not dead, is he? How creepy would that be?"

"He's breathing."

"I'm going to take his sunglasses off."

"Why?"

Sephie removed the old man's dark glasses.

"I knew it, he's not deaf and he's not dead, he's sleeping."

"Wake him up."

Sephie shook his shoulder a little harder.

"He won't wake up."

Odo poked him in the ribs. "Wakey wakey, old man! Pokey pokey! Blueberry pancakes for breakfast today! You snooze, you lose!"

"Odo, don't be rude."

"I'm just trying to wake him."

Silas grinned. "Is that how your mommy wakes you? Wakey wakey, little Odo!"

"Only on school days."

Silas grabbed the man's foot, shaking it. The old man's snoring grew louder.

Odo stared at him. "There has to be some weird special way to wake him up. Maybe we're supposed to slap him really hard."

"Odo, please. You're not slapping an old sleeping man."

Emmy cried out, "I know what to do!"

Chapter 25

The Sleeper Awakens

Emmy grinned. "Okay, class, can anyone tell me what the Sleeper is doing?"

Odo raised his hand. "He's sleeping. Do I get an A?"

"Excellent answer, but not the right one, I'm afraid. Anyone else?"

Silas grinned. "He's snoring like Odo does?"

Sephie raised her hand. "He's fishing!"

"Exactly, and what would wake up a fisherman?"

Sephie stepped over to the edge of the dock, gently tugging on the nylon fishing line.

The old man made a loud snorting, gasping noise, his eyes opening. He looked at the four friends, croaking out, "More back roaders?"

The wall of fog had vanished.

Odo said, "What's a back roader?"

The old man gave him a disgusted look. "It's people like you who skip the Central Admin Main Import Distribution Terminal, lazy people who can't be bothered with such bureaucratic nonsense. Here's a clue, pipsqueak, the world couldn't exist without organized bureaucracy, it's what keeps the trains running."

Odo was pretty sure there weren't any trains here, but decided not to mention that. "We didn't mean to skip that Terminal place, but we got lost. We arrived in Arcadia, then walked to South Elysium. Someone told us we had to wake you."

The old man eyed Odo suspiciously. "How did you get to Arcadia?"

Odo glanced at Sephie, then said, "Well, funny story, I'm actually translucent and we were dimensional shifting using a waystone when we–"

"You're shifters? You don't belong here! What were you thinking, nimbus? Wait, you're not dead are you?"

Odo's jaw tightened. "We're not dead, not even almost dead. We're trying to get to the River Styx. We have to talk to Charon the Ferryman."

The old man gave a loud snort. "Why would you want to talk to that old geezer? He's older than I am and twice as crazy. Let's see your papers, back roader."

"Papers?"

"Are you deaf, nimbus? Show me your Free Passage Certificates, and they'd better be signed and stamped and dated and signed again."

Odo nodded, smiling brightly. "Of course, our Free Passage Certificates. Might I have one moment to confer with my three associates regarding our Free Passage Certificates?"

The old man scowled. "Don't try to bamboozle me with your fancy words, you little nimmy. You have one minute before I go back to sleep."

Odo turned to Sephie, whispering, "Can you shape some fake papers for him?"

"I have no idea what they look like, Odo."

"What are we going to do?"

Silas whispered, "Let's make a run for it, hop in the boat and row past the fog while he's still awake."

"There's no time, his eyes are drooping already."

Sephie grinned. "I have an idea." There was a flash of blue light, a tall white cup appearing in her hand.

"What's that?"

"You'll see." Sephie stepped over to the old man. "Have you ever tried a sixteen ounce double pumpkin spice flat white latte with triple microfoam and four shots of espresso? So good."

"I'm not thirsty. I don't get thirsty. Where are your papers?"

"Just smell it, it's so good. You don't have to be thirsty to enjoy it." She held it under his nose.

"Smells good, reminds me of pumpkin pie, had it when I was a kid every– wait, is this a trick? Are you trying to poison me?"

Sephie took a sip. "Mmm, so good. Tastes like pumpkin pie on Christmas day."

The old man shrugged, reaching out for the cup. "I'll try a sip. Then I want your papers. If you think you can bribe me, you're dead wrong, missy."

"I know we can't bribe you, but it never hurts to be nice to people. Kindness is its own reward, I always say."

The old man grunted, taking a sip. "Not bad. Kind of tasty." He proceeded to chug the entire sixteen ounce super caffeinated pumpkin spice espresso latte, letting out a loud belch when he was done.

Odo whispered, "Whoa, no way, he drank the whole thing."

The old man's eyes were shining bright. "I like it, I feel good, wide awake, I feel great, I might go for a walk, maybe a run, maybe jump on a trampoline, there must be one around here somewhere, maybe I could make a trampoline out of my chair, maybe I can build a skateboard ramp with a–"

Sephie hollered, "Everyone in the boat!"

The four friends jumped in, pushing off from the dock, Odo and Silas grabbing the oars.

"It's showtime!"

Odo glared at Sephie. "You can't always be the one who decides whether it's showtime or not."

"Less talking, more rowing!"

The old man was jumping up and down on the dock, shaking his fist at them. "Come back here! Show me your papers, you little whippersnappers!"

Ten minutes later they had rounded a curve in the river, leaving the highly agitated and wide awake Sleeper behind them.

Emmy laughed. "That was brilliant! He won't sleep for a week after all that coffee."

Odo set his oars down, leaning back in his seat. "It was kind of a brilliant idea. I was worried there for a minute, he seemed kind of crazy."

"You think?"

They drifted lazily down the river for almost an hour, past lush forests and magnificent gardens, listening to the colorful birds chirping and tweeting.

"This is paradise, so beautiful."

Odo squinted, looking ahead. "What's that weird little building down there?"

"It looks like an old abandoned shack."

"The grass is all brown around it, no leaves on the trees. There's trash in the yard."

"Creepy. Maybe it's haunted. Do you think they have haunted houses here?"

"I haven't seen any ghosts."

"Wait, if they have houses in the Land of the Dead, wouldn't they all be haunted houses because ghosts live in them?"

Sephie ignored Odo's question. "Row us closer, there's a sign in front of it."

Odo let out a yelp when he read the sign. "We have to stop here! We have to!"

Magnificent Madam Malitia
World Renowned Fortune Teller Extraordinaire
What amazing secrets does **your** future hold?
FREE Consultations!
Complimentary Donuts!

Chapter 26

Madam Malitia

"We're not stopping, Odo. I can tell you right now, Madam Malitia is a fraud. Just look at the sign, look at the yard. Complimentary donuts? Do you think a world renowned fortune teller would live in a run down shack in the middle of nowhere and offer free donuts?"

"World renowned fortune tellers aren't like regular people, Sephie. They don't care about money and big houses and fancy gardens. They're thinking about stuff that happens in the future, not stuff happening now."

"You mean she's thinking about how happy she'll be in the future when she gets all your money? Besides, your future depends on your actions, on the choices you make. You already know that, Odo Whitley. What's wrong with you?"

"Nothing's wrong with me, Sephie. What happens if I'm walking down the street humming a catchy tune and a giant asteroid lands on my head? Getting squished by the asteroid had nothing to do with the choices I made, but Madam Malitia could warn me to watch out for asteroids on a certain day. That's how it works."

"She's a fraud."

"She's not some phony fortune teller in a shady traveling carnival; she lives on the Summerland River near the River Styx. She's not a fraud, she's the real thing."

Sephie pressed her hand to her forehead, giving an exasperated groan. "Fine, we'll go see Madam Malitia, but don't come crying to me when she takes all your money and tells you she sees good things in your future and you're going to meet a certain special someone in six months."

Silas looked at Emmy with a grin, rowing the boat over to the rickety wooden dock. This was going to be hilarious. "Here we are." He hopped out, studying the decrepit old shack. "Odo, I hate to say it, but Sephie might be right about–"

Odo strode past Silas, rapping loudly on the front door.

A gravelly voice called out, "Come in, I have been expecting you."

Odo turned to Sephie with a triumphant smile. "She's been expecting us. I told you she was the real thing."

"You need to get your neural synapses adjusted, Odo Whitley. She says that every time there's a knock on her door."

Odo pushed the door open, eyeing the old gray

haired woman seated at the crooked table, a large crystal ball in front of her. She wore a purple robe covered with indecipherable gold symbols, enormous black glasses, and bright red shoes.

She put a hand to her temple when the four friends stepped in. "Yes, yes, it is just as I saw it this morning. Four visitors from far away, two boys and two girls. One of them was wearing a green striped shirt, one girl had flaming orange hair. It is just as I predicted."

Odo nodded, "Whoa, that's amazing. You even knew about Sephie's orange hair."

Madam Malitia held up one hand. "Wait, I am sensing something, a name, it starts with... an s, a short name... is it Sarah, no... Sophie... not quite... Sephie, that's it! Is one of you named Sephie?"

"That's incredible, you knew Sephie's name! She's the one with orange hair."

"Just as I predicted."

Sephie groaned. Odo had said Sephie's name five seconds before Madam Malitia pretended to guess it.

Odo took a seat in front of Madam Malitia. "I'd like to get my fortune told."

"First comes your consultation, no charge of course, as advertised. Unfortunately, as I predicted exactly three weeks ago to the day, we are out of complimentary donuts."

"That's fine, we're not hungry anyway."

"Excellent." She waved her hands slowly in the air, murmuring strange foreign sounding words in a soft sing song voice. She lowered her head, her eyes focused on the crystal ball.

"Ahh, all is clear. I see it now in the crystal ball. Four friends traveling down the Summerland River in a wooden boat. I see them from above, on their way to... the River Styx?"

"Yes, exactly right! That's amazing. We're going there to see Charon the Ferryman."

"Yes, I foresaw that only yesterday, you are on your way to see Charon the Ferryman. You are going there to see him about... something he wants?"

"Yes, the Key Spike, we're taking it to him."

Malitia let out a loud gasp, "I see it clearly now! Charon's ferry is damaged, something is missing, the ferry isn't working. It's black, long and sharp. It's... it's... the Key Spike! The spike stolen from him by Odysseus! You have found it, just as I predicted you would!"

Odo turned, looking at the others. "She knew about the Key Spike and she knew about Odysseus!"

Sephie, Silas, and Emmy stared at Odo. Silas' mouth was hanging open. What was wrong with Odo?

"What? I told you she was a real fortune teller."

Madam Malitia got to her feet, her eyes half closed. "It is time to read your fortune, but first I must ring the sacred prophecy gong three times!"

She clanged a large brass gong hanging from the ceiling, suddenly looking like she was going to faint. "I'm weak, so weak. I see it all. This is bad, very bad."

"What's bad, what do you see? Am I going to die? Is it time already?" Odo's face was pale, his hands shaking.

Sephie was getting a bad feeling. Is it time? Was he going to die? What did that mean?

"I see two men wearing green cloaks; they are going to rob you! They are dangerous men armed with deadly daggers. You must do exactly as they say or you will be MURDERED WHERE YOU STAND!"

Odo jumped to his feet, his eyes wide. "Who are they?"

"They're my two boys, Ozzie and Bobo!" She let out a shrieking laugh, pointing to the door.

The door swung open, two burly men wearing tattered green cloaks stepping inside, one of them with a long scraggly black beard. The other one pulled a vicious looking dagger from his belt.

Madam Malitia hollered, "Grab the boy's pack, he has Charon's lost Key Spike! It's worth a fortune! Get it!"

Sephie drew two quick symbols in the air, but nothing happened.

Madam Malitia gave another horrible screeching laugh. "No powers allowed in my house, dearie! Tie up her hands nice and tight before you take her outside."

One of the men grabbed Odo's pack, pulling the Key Spike out. "Got it, Ma! Should I send him to the Land of the Dead?" He gave a sinister laugh, eyeing Odo.

"Throw them in the boat, send them down the river. We'll be long gone before they get back. Thanks for the spike, dearie. I see wonderful things in your future. You'll meet that special someone in six months!" She let out a shrieking laugh, grabbing the spike and running out the back door.

The scraggly bearded man in the green cloak held his dagger to Odo's throat. "Everyone in the boat or your friend wakes up in the Land of the Dead."

One of the men grabbed the oars from the boat, tossing them into the yard. "In the boat, all of you!"

As their boat drifted down the Summerland River, three sets of eyes were on Odo.

"What? Why are you looking at me like that?"

Chapter 27

Odo's Secret

"Untie my hands."

Odo loosened the ropes around Sephie's wrists, dropping them to the floor of the boat. "Sorry, it was my fault."

Sephie studied his unhappy face. "Odo Whitley, you have to tell me what's wrong. Why did you want to see the fortune teller? She was clearly a fraud, anyone could see that."

Odo looked down at his feet.

"Odo?"

"I wanted her to be real. I wanted to know the truth."

"The truth about what?"

Odo turned away again.

Silas put his hand on Odo's shoulder. "You can tell us anything, you know that. We're all pals, all superheroes."

"I wanted to know how soon it's going to happen."

"What's going to happen?"

"How soon until I die."

"Why would you even say that? Is something wrong?"

Odo held out his hand, palm facing up. "That's what's wrong."

Sephie studied his hand. "What am I looking at? It's just your hand."

Odo pointed to the little creases on his palm.

"Right there. It's bad."

"I still don't see it, you have to tell me exactly what's wrong."

"When I was eight years old my mom told me she went to a palm reader when she was young and they said she was going to meet a special someone and then six months later she met my dad. I wanted to learn about palm reading, to understand how it worked, so I borrowed a book from the library. When I read my palm I found something really bad. My life line and fate lines are really, really short. I measured them and figured out I would probably die before I was eighteen, maybe sooner. I wanted Madam Malitia to tell me exactly how much time I have left. It's probably a year at the most."

Sephie glanced over at Silas and Emmy. Silas had his hand over his mouth, his eyes wide. It looked like he was trying desperately not to laugh.

Sephie took Odo's hand in hers. "You're saying you think you're going to die because you read your palm when you were eight years old and your life line is short?"

Odo held out his hand. "Look at it, look how short

those two lines are. I don't have much longer."

Sephie blinked. "Now that I'm looking at it, it does look short. I had no idea. I'm a little confused though. Could you explain the science behind reading palms? How the wrinkle lines that form when your little baby hands are scrunched up inside your mom have anything at all to do with how long you're going to live? Could you explain the physiology behind that, the biological connection between the human life span and the little wrinkly lines on your hands? It's really confusing to me."

"It's not an exact science, it's palm reading. They look at the lines and they can tell stuff about your life. It's probably more of an art than a science."

She grabbed his hand, studying it. "Oh, no, do you see this line? This curvy one?"

"What is it? What does it mean?"

"It means you're an idiot, Odo Whitley. You were eight years old and you read a book about palm reading and scared yourself silly because you didn't know anything about science or physiology or physics or neural pathways or–"

"The book said my life line was really short."

"The book said that? And who wrote the book?"

"I don't know, a palm reading lady. I think her name was Madam Futura."

"A palm reading lady named Madam Futura?"

Odo nodded.

Sephie said, "When I was little I used to be afraid I would get sucked down the bathtub drain. I had to get out of the tub before my mom drained it. You were a kid, Odo Whitley, and kids believe some pretty weird things. It's time to let it go. You were a kid and you were wrong. You were very wrong."

Silas grinned. "I never wanted to be an actor because I thought when actors died on a TV show they really died."

Emmy said, "I thought people on TV could hear what I was saying so I was always really polite when the TV was on."

Odo was silent for a long time. "I guess if I think about it, it is kind of goofy to think a book about palm reading could tell me when I was going to die. I guess I never really questioned it, I believed it for so long that it was real to me. I thought it was going to happen no matter what I did."

"Emmy said, "No one can possibly know how long they're going to live. They just can't."

Silas knew she was talking about Jacob.

Sephie said, "Just because you believe something for a long time doesn't mean it's true. Plenty of good people believe things with all their heart that aren't true, some for their whole lives. Think about all the people in ancient Greece who believed that Zeus threw lightning bolts. They were all wrong, Odo Whitley. All of them. They weren't bad people, they just didn't have all the facts. Neither did you when you read Madam Futura's book."

Odo nodded. "I guess we should probably figure out how to get the Key Spike back from Madam Malitia.

Since I'm not dying just yet."

Sephie laughed. "I've got this, Odo Whitley."

Sephie drew two symbols in the air and a pair of wooden oars blinked in existence.

Emmy said, "That's so amazing. You're like a wizard."

"It's just science."

Silas grabbed the oars. "What's our plan?"

A second pair of oars appeared. "You and Odo are going to row us back to Madam Malitia's house. We'll track them from there and get the spike back."

Odo took a seat behind Silas, slipping the oars into the oar locks. "Ready."

The two friends turned the boat around, heading upriver, a task which proved far easier than they had anticipated.

"This is great, my arms don't get tired at all, even rowing as hard as I can."

As they rounded a bend in the river, Emmy called out, "There it is! I see her house!"

They tied up at the dock, heading into Madam Malitia's decrepit little shack.

"How are we going to track them? They could have gone anywhere."

"We use logic. They know the spike belongs to Charon, so they must be heading to the River Styx. We didn't see another boat, so we know they're walking, and we know it has to be on this side of the river."

"Let's check inside, see if we can find any clues, maybe a map or something."

Emmy pushed the door open, stepping inside. "It smells like stinky old shoes in here."

Odo stepped behind Madam Malitia's table, his eyes on the crystal ball. "I wonder if this thing really works?" He gazed into the orb, giving a loud gasp.

"What is it?"

Odo waved his arms slowly in the air. "All is clear! I can see it now, just as I predicted five years ago. I see… I see…Silas meeting that certain special someone… he's on a school bus… and, wait, I see someone else meeting her special someone on the same day… I can see her face now, it's a girl, and she's sitting next to–"

"Knock it off, Odo Whitley, it's not funny."

Silas grinned. Emmy's face was bright red.

"Just being my normal hilarious self." Odo pulled a drawer open, eyeing the mishmash of miscellaneous household junk. He pulled a wooden box from the back of the drawer, reading the label. "Whoa! Look at this!"

Chapter 28

Memories

Sephie stepped over to the table, Odo pointing to the handwritten label on the box.

Waystones

"Madam Malitia is a shifter?"

"She has waystones, she must be."

"That would explain how they got here."

Silas nodded. "They're probably hiding out from all the angry people who didn't meet their certain special someone."

Odo laughed, opening the box. "They're labeled, but I don't recognize any of them. Except for South Elysium. That's what she used to get here. Should we take them?"

"Put them in your pack. We don't want her to use them to escape. We'll have to be careful, she could be far more dangerous than we thought, maybe a Fortisian."

Odo frowned. "Suppose she has crazy powers like

Cyra and can vaporize us?"

Sephie closed the box of waystones. "Good point. We probably can't use brute force against her, so we'll have to trick her."

"How?"

"I'm thinking."

"Can you cloud her thoughts or something?"

"Something like that, but I don't know how strong her powers are. Okay, I have a plan, but I'll need your help."

"What do I have to do?"

"You have to let me read your memories."

"You mean look at my brainwaves?"

Sephie shook her head. "No, it's deeper than that, something Cyra taught me on Plindor. I have to merge my mind with yours, then rummage around in your memories until I find what I'm looking for."

Odo frowned. "You'll see all my memories, even the embarrassing ones?"

"It's me, Odo Whitley, your best friend in the world. You'll be able to see all my memories too, even embarrassing ones. Like the first time I saw you and gave you that note. And the first time I knew how much I liked you."

Odo said, "Fine, enough about that stuff. Do whatever you have to do." He glanced over at Silas and Emmy, both of them grinning.

Sephie pressed her hand against the right side of Odo's head. "It shouldn't take too long. I know exactly which memory I'm looking for."

Odo's eyes were suddenly vacant.

Silas whispered, "Whoa, that's weird. He looks like a zombie. So does Sephie."

Odo was sitting at his desk in science class. "What is this?" He turned, gulping when he saw himself at the desk next to him, his eyes riveted to a book on neuro-physiology. "This is Sephie's memory! This is when she gave me that first note."

A thought popped into his head. "He's kind of cute. Really shy though, probably because he's translucent. Uh oh, he knows I'm staring at him, his brainwaves are flaring like crazy, especially his amygdala. He's scared silly. He probably thinks I'm going to talk to him or something. He's so funny. Now he's fixing his hair. He's embarrassed, thinks that's what I'm looking at. He has nice hair, not crazy orange hair like me. I like him. He's really smart and he'd be fun to talk to once he got over being so afraid of me. If he wanted to talk to me. He might not want to. I wonder if he knows some people call me Creepy Crumb? I hope not. I don't want him to think I'm creepy. I don't feel creepy, but he might think I was. I'll write him a note so he knows I care about his brain, not his hair." Odo looked down, watching his hands write the note.

It's not your hair, it's what's under it

"Whoa, she liked me the first time she saw me. I thought she'd think I was totally weird or something. I thought she was really cute too. I always liked her orange hair."

"Thanks, Odo."

Odo gave a screech, "You can hear what I'm thinking?"

"Of course I can, our minds are merged."

"I guess it's okay that you know I thought you were cute. And that I liked your hair."

"I'm glad you thought that, Odo Whitley. I was so embarrassed about it, and about people calling me Creepy Crumb. I was afraid you would make fun of me."

"I would never do that."

"I know that now, it just took a while for me to trust you."

"Me too. You were my first real friend. Did you find the memory you needed?"

"I did. Ready to go back to the real world?"

"I guess so. This is kind of fun though. It's easier to talk to you here about embarrassing stuff."

Silas watched the light returned to Odo's eyes.

Odo said, "That was so weird! I was seeing memories through Sephie's eyes, and she could hear what I was thinking."

Silas grinned. "What kind of memories, Odo?"

"Oh, you know, the none of your business kind?"

Sephie headed for the door. "We have to hurry, we need to catch them before they reach Charon."

"We should run. I don't think Madam Malitia moves too fast."

The four friends took off, racing along the Summerland River, streaking through glorious lush forests and bucolic open meadows.

Odo hollered, "I think I saw something shiny back there in the grass! It could have been something valuable, like a gold coin."

"No time for that! We have to catch Madam Malitia. We can't bring Jacob back without the Key Spike."

"I know that, but–"

Sephie hollered, "Run faster!"

Odo's legs were a blur as they raced up a long hill through a wide swath of blue wildflowers, entering into a dense forest of magnificent towering ancient trees. "It's a redwood forest! These trees are amazing! Look how tall they–"

He skidded to a halt, scrunching down behind one of the gigantic trees, the others following suit.

"What is it? Did you see something?"

"I caught a glimpse of someone up ahead. Maybe they set up camp for the night. It's getting dark."

"It's weird that there's no sun in the sky, but they still have night and day here. It's like the whole sky just lights up."

Sephie closed her eyes. "I'll be back in a minute, I'm going to use the Traveling Eye."

Five minutes later she opened her eyes. "It's them. You were right, they set up camp. Stay low and follow me."

The four friends crawled silently through the under-growth, stopping to listen, watching for any movement ahead of them.

Finally Sephie stopped, motioning for them to lie still, pointing through the tall spiky grass. Odo could see Madam Malitia and her two sons sitting in front of a campfire.

Sephie whispered, "I'm going to create illusions that will seem real to them. They'll see them and hear them, but they won't really exist. I'll send them to you guys too, so you can see what they're seeing. Don't do anything or say anything, no matter what you see. Stay silent."

Chapter 29

Sephie's Plan

Sephie drew nine complex symbols in the air, a crashing noise sounding in the forest. Odo watched Madam Malitia and her two sons jump up, Ozzie and Bobo pulling out their daggers.

"What is that? Who's there?"

Madam Malitia hollered, "Eyes open! Look sharp, boys!"

Odo instantly recognized Charon the Ferryman when he stepped into the clearing in his ragged brown robe, his cold black eyes coming to rest on Malitia and her sons.

One of the sons yelled, "It's him! It's Charon!"

Madam Malitia motioned for them to lower their daggers.

"Greetings, Charon the Ferryman, I am pleased that destiny has brought us together. We were on our way to the River Styx to see you. "

Charon roared, "I know you have it! Give it to me or you will find yourself in the Land of the Dead."

Madam Malitia gave a sickly sweet smile. "Of

course, Charon, that was always our intention, to return the Key Spike to you as quickly as possible."

"Give it to me, then. The reward is known to all, you will be allowed to bring one soul back from the Land of the Dead to the Land of the Living. Who will it be? Be quick about it, give me a name."

"Strangely enough, dear Charon, we have no desire to bring anyone back from the Land of the Dead. Perhaps we might settle on some other form of remuneration?"

"What do you want? Spit it out, speak plainly. The dead wait impatiently to cross the River Styx."

"I thought perhaps something simple, like a thousand gold coins. Certainly the return of your Key Spike is worth that much to you."

Charon waved one hand, a deafening clap of thunder sounding, a large wood and silver chest blinking into existence. He pulled a heavy gold key from his cloak, unlocking the chest. Madam Malitia's eyes gleamed, licking her lips at the sight of ten thousand shiny gold coins.

"More than generous, Charon. The Key Spike is yours."

Charon gave a cold, humorless laugh. "Ten gold coins is what you get. No more."

Madam Malitia's expression turned to ice. "I'll take the whole chest or the Key Spike is gone forever, melted into a glowing blob of iron!"

Flames sprouted from Charon's hands, his voice shaking the ground around him. "Ten gold coins or you and your hideous offspring will be turned to ash!"

Madam Malitia took a step back, her sickly sweet smile returning. "Perhaps in my haste to return the spike, I have badly misjudged its value. Fair is fair, I agree to your terms, ten gold coins for the return of your lost Key Spike."

"Give it to me, then you get the coins."

"Of course. Fair is fair." Madam Malitia reached into her pocket, pulling out the black spike. "Here it is, your precious Key Spike." She raised her arm, then shrieked, "Now go get it!"

She hurled the spike as far as she could into the dense undergrowth. With a roar, Charon charged into the forest after the spike.

Madam Malitia hollered, "Ozzie! Bobo! Now!"

She ran over to the chest of gold coins, touching it with one hand, her sons grabbing her arm. She pulled an amulet from her pocket, shouting to Charon, "I'm as rich as Croesus thanks to you, you old fool!" There was a brilliant flash of blue light, then silence. Madam Malitia, her two sons, and the chest of gold coins had vanished.

Sephie had a wide grin. "We did it! Let's go get the spike!"

"Wait, what happened? Did she get the gold coins?"

"I used your memory of Charon the Ferryman to create his image, then I used Madam Malitia's own greed against her. I showed her the huge chest of gold coins, telling her she could only have ten coins. It made her furious that I had so many but would only give her a few. She wanted them all, and the only way for her to get them was to shift out of here with the chest."

Odo said, "She can't come back because we have her South Elysium waystone."

"Exactly. And by now, wherever she is, she has discovered the chest of gold coins was an illusion, existing only in her mind."

Odo pressed his hand to his temple. "All is clear, I see it now, just as I predicted one hundred years ago! Madam Malitia is jumping up and down, screaming out lots of extremely rude words."

Silas laughed. "You are correct, Odo the Magnificent."

It took them half an hour to find the spike, Emmy giving a shout, holding it up. "Found it!"

Odo said, "I just thought of something, right before she shifted she said she told Charon she was as rich as Croesus. What does that mean?"

Silas said, "Croesus was the king of Lydia in ancient Greece. He was wealthier than any other king before him, becoming quite a legend. I think he ruled Lydia from 585 to 545BC. It was a common expression for a long time to say someone was as rich as Croesus."

"You just happened to know that?"

"I guess. I read a lot of history books."

Emmy said, "I think that's amazing."

Silas grinned. "Thanks."

Odo stood up, brushing the leaves and dirt from his clothes. "So what now? We head for the River Styx?"

"We do. We'll hike along the river, look for a boat."

"Let's camp here for the night and leave in the morning. They have a nice campfire going, and they left all their camping gear."

Sephie grinned, "I could shape some chocolate, graham crackers, and marshmallows."

"Yum, you don't have to be hungry to like s'mores."

The four friends sat around the campfire, eating s'mores and laughing about how they had outwitted Madam Malitia. Odo, Sephie, and Silas told Emmy about some of their adventures on Atroxia and Emerus, Odo describing in great detail Sephie's amazing powers.

Four hours later, a soft voice woke Emmy.

"We are pleased with you."

Her eyes popped open. The voice was in her mind, but it wasn't Nomi's. She sensed it was coming from the forest. She crawled out of her sleeping bag, standing up, peering into the murky woods, spotting a curious glow coming from behind one of the trees.

She called out, "Hello?"

"This way, child. I don't wish to wake the others."

Under any other circumstances, a mysterious voice from an unknown being in a shadowy forest would have terrified her, but there was something about the voice, something true, something good. She crept to the edge of the clearing, then stepped around a massive tree trunk, her eyes on an impossibly strange being.

"What are you?"

Chapter 30

Emmy's Revelation

"We are pleased with you."

Emmy studied the glowing white creature floating six inches above the forest floor, with its long ropy arms, bulbous head, no eyes, ears, or mouth.

"Who are you?"

"I am a Sinarian."

"Are you an angel?"

"I am not. I am a living being, no different than you."

Emmy decided not to comment on their obvious differences.

"I am aware you are able to fly in your dreams."

"It took me a while to learn how, but once I realized there were no laws of physics in dreams, I could do whatever I wanted to. When I dream, my legs are straight and nothing can hurt me."

"Most people have dreams without being aware they are dreaming. This is not the case for you?"

"I learned how to wake up in my dreams. I know I'm having a dream, and I know my real physical body is home in bed sleeping."

"I see. This is most admirable. You are capable of flight in dreams, but not in the real world?"

Emmy nodded. "I've tried to fly in the real world but I can't."

"When you are dreaming, are all the objects in your dream floating about because there is no gravity, no laws of physics?"

"No, and that's a little odd, now that I think about it. I know there isn't gravity in dreams because I can fly, but everything else seems to be obeying the laws of physics. Except nothing can hurt me, objects pass right through me."

"Curious, indeed."

Emmy sensed the Sinarian did not find it curious at all. He was trying to teach her something by asking her questions.

"You are correct, I am trying to teach you a deeper truth."

"What kind of truth?"

"What would you say is the main difference between a dream world and a real world?"

Emmy thought for a moment. "It's kind of hard to say. The dream worlds seem real to me; I can touch things, see things, smell things, but I know it's a dream. Sometimes a dream world can seem so real that I have to test it by trying to fly. If I can fly, then I know it's a dream world."

"What would you say if I told you the worlds you have been visiting are not dream worlds, but real ones?"

Emmy laughed. "That's not possible. I can't fly in real worlds. I know I can't."

"Again, most curious."

Emmy stared at the Sinarian. "I don't understand what you're trying to teach me."

"If I am correct, and you were indeed visiting real worlds as you slept, what would explain your ability to fly?"

"Um… the body I had in those worlds would have to be different than my real physical body. I was creating a different body in that world, one that could fly?"

"Ah, now we're getting somewhere. You were creating a new body with your mind. You were creating a body capable of flight. But you weren't doing it in a dream, you were doing it in real worlds. That would indeed explain you ability to fly."

"Except it's not possible."

"And yet you have done it many dozens of times."

"I don't like this. It's scary."

"I want you to try something. I will help you."

"Try what?"

"Imagine this is one of your dream worlds, then try to fly."

"But I know it's not."

"Pretend it is. I will help you pretend."

The Sinarian waved his arm slowly back and forth in front of Emmy, her eyes closing. *"Awaken in your*

182

dream."

Emmy's eyes opened. "You made me dream?"

"Look at your legs."

"They're straight. Am I dreaming?"

"Are you?"

"I don't know."

"Change your body back to its original form. Visualize your crooked legs, imagine this is a very real world."

Emmy stared at her legs, concentrating. Her jaw dropped when she saw them transform. They were crooked again.

"Excellent. Now make them straight."

She stared at her legs, watching them become straight and strong. "This is amazing, I can really do it."

"Excellent. Now fly."

"What?"

"Transform your body into one that can fly. There's nothing to it, you've done it many times already in absolutely real worlds."

Emmy imagined she was in a dream world, giving herself permission to fly because there were no laws of physics, no gravity.

Ten seconds later she floated up from the forest floor, her eyes on the Sinarian. "Is this real? Am I really flying in a real world?"

"It is, and you are. It is why the four of you have been brought together. I want you to practice flying for an hour, get used to the idea that you can fly, make it feel normal, just the way things are, the way the world

works, like taking a stroll outside. Birds can fly, so can you. It's just life, nothing strange, it's all quite ordinary, almost tedious. There is one other thing I must request of you at this time."

"What?"

"Under no circumstances are you to tell the others you can fly."

"Why?"

"Because I am asking you not to tell them. There are many forces at work of which you have no understanding, no awareness. It is for your own good, and the safety of your friends that I ask this of you. If you tell them, or show them your ability, the power will be taken from you. Do you understand? You will never fly again. Ever."

"I won't tell them because I don't want anything to happen to them."

"Excellent. I am leaving now. There is presently enough light for you to see. Fly for an hour, then return."

"I don't understand why I can fly, but they can't."

"Because you know how to fly and they don't."

"I know, but…"

"We will speak again."

The Sinarian was there, and then he was not.

Emmy was floating three feet above the ground.

"He's gone, and I can still fly. This is real, it's not a dream."

She shot up into the sky, soaring across the treetops, just as she had done so many times before.

"It's so beautiful up here." She spotted a light in the distance. "What is that? It looks like a big flame."

She streaked toward the light, arriving moments later, her eyes on a small town surrounding a great rectangular stone structure.

"It beautiful, it looks like an ancient Roman temple."

She flew lower, studying the massive marble structure with its classic pillars, a thirty-foot tall orange flame spouting out of its gleaming stone portico. A dozen people wearing yellow tunics were pouring liquid from clay pots into a circle of holes surrounding the flame.

"That must be fuel to keep the flame going. It's some kind of sacred eternal flame, but what is it doing here? Why is there an ancient Roman town here? What is this place?"

She flew on, spotting other towns and villages from a multitude of different eras, some ancient, some current, some with highly advanced futuristic technology.

"This is confusing. I should head back."

She flew toward the Summerland River, spotting a wooden boat washed up on the shore only a mile from where they were camping.

"Perfect, we can use that boat. I'll make sure we walk along the river bank and find it."

She landed in the forest at the edge of the clearing, checking to make sure no one was up. She concentrated on her legs, watching them transform, her awkward gait returning.

Ten minutes later she was curled up in her sleeping bag, her mind spinning. She could fly. For better or worse, her world had changed forever.

Chapter 31

Bob the Mechanic

"Odo, get up, you're going to be late for school!"

Odo groaned, rolling over in his sleeping bag. "I'm almost dressed, Mom." He remembered where he was when he heard Silas and Sephie laughing. He glared at them. "Very funny."

"We've been up for almost an hour. We're going to hike along the Summerland River, watch for boats, maybe get a ride from someone."

"A ride with some weird alien robot fortune teller who wants to stab us and steal the Key Spike?"

Silas laughed, then said, "As crazy as that sounds, Odo does have a point. Maybe we should keep a low profile until we get the spike to Charon."

Emmy grabbed her backpack, slinging it onto her shoulder. "Maybe we'll find a boat or something."

Sephie nodded, stopping when she noticed something peculiar about Emmy's brainwaves. "Good idea. We can leave the camping gear here. I can shape whatever we need along the way."

Odo raised his hand. "Just so you know, I usually

sleep on a big pile of gold coins, so if you could shape me a chest full of–"

"Nice try, Odo Whitley. You know the rules, no shaping for personal gain."

"So unfair."

"Let's go!"

"Is it showtime?"

"We're strolling along a beautiful river on a lovely warm day. Does that sound like showtime to you?"

As they headed through the towering redwoods, Odo said, "I've been thinking."

"That never ends well."

"I've been thinking that our group needs a name. I know we can't give Emmy her superhero name until we get home, but we could give the group a name."

Sephie gave Odo a dubious look. "I'm guessing you thought of one?"

"As a matter of fact, I have. I'd like to run it past you and see what you think, get some first impressions."

"What is it?"

"The Amazing Translucent Boy and his Three Sidekicks. What do you think?"

Silas furrowed his brow. "Interesting, very interesting. I'm trying to decide if we should take turns punching you, or all of us punch you simultaneously."

Sephie laughed. "I'll go first!"

Odo grinned. "Fine, I'll think of something else."

"It would be kind of cool if we had a name, though."

"Why do we need one? Nobody knows we exist, no one knows about our powers."

"Okay, just imagine us arriving on a strange world and a bunch of aliens start jumping up and down, pointing at us, saying, 'No way, it's *The Amazing Translucent Boy and his Three Sidekicks*!'"

"Never say those words again, Odo Whitley."

Emmy laughed.

They reached the end of the forest trail, the Summerland River coming into view.

"It's such a beautiful river. Do you think there are fish in it?"

"I haven't seen any wildlife except birds. This place is odd."

"On the bright side there's no deadly alien monsters trying to eat us."

"True."

Emmy was walking ahead of them, Sephie studying her brainwaves. They had changed, her brain flaring in places where it shouldn't be, but she wasn't sure what it meant. It didn't match anything she'd seen in her brain mapping studies.

Emmy suddenly ran ahead, calling out, "I found a boat!"

The others raced down the trail, catching up to her.

"It's better than the one we had. It has a little cabin."

"And it has oars. We're good to go."

"I wonder whose boat it is? We probably shouldn't take it, the owner might be coming back."

"It's covered with dead leaves, it looks abandoned. It probably broke free and floated down the river. We can always return it later."

Odo climbed on board, stepping over to the cabin. "I'll see if there's any–" He gave a screech, stumbling backwards out of the doorway.

"What is it? What's in there?"

Odo pointed mutely, a man wearing greasy blue coveralls and a ragged San Diego Padres hat stepping out onto the deck.

"It's Mike the Mechanic!"

The man turned to him, studying him like a curious bug he had discovered on his kitchen floor. "You know those round things in your face? They're called eyes. You might try using them sometime, sonny boy."

It all came rushing back to him, Odo remembering why Mike the Mechanic had been so fantastically annoying. He decided then and there not to put up with his rude, sarcastic, condescending behavior. He would go on the offensive. "What are you jabbering on about? And what are you doing on our boat? Take a hike, pal."

The man in the blue coveralls did not remove his gaze from Odo, pointing instead with one long finger to an embroidered patch on his coveralls. "I can read it out loud if there are too many letters for you."

Odo eyed the patch. "Bob? Your name is Bob? Why did you change it, too many bill collectors chasing you?" He looked at Sephie, grinning. That was a good one. Burn.

"I didn't change my name, Mr. Nimbus. *I can't believe you don't know that. Everyone knows that.*"

A chill shot through Odo. That's what his dad always said. *I can't believe you don't know that. Everyone knows that.* How could Bob or Mike or whatever his name was possibly know that? Unless he was reading Odo's thoughts. He decided to take a different tact.

"You're really Bob the Mechanic? That's amazing, because we met someone who looks exactly like you in Palusia. He had the same uniform and everything. What a strange coincidence."

"Very strange." He stared at Odo, his eyes vibrating slightly.

"What are you doing with your eyes? What is that?"

"I'm wondering if you're the one who pushed the big red button when you were clearly instructed not to."

"Oh, right, that. Well, funny story, we went in–"

"I hope you have a good attorney and lots of money, deep pockets."

"Wait, what? Why?"

"What are you doing on my boat?"

"This is your boat?"

"I was here first, ipso facto, it's my boat. You're trespassing, sonny boy. I could have you arrested."

"Maybe we got off to a bad start. Let's try again. Hi, my name is Odo, and these are my three friends, Silas, Sephie–"

"So boring, I'm falling asleep. Do you have any coffee? Maybe a sixteen ounce double pumpkin spice flat white latte with triple microfoam and four shots of espresso?"

Odo grimaced. He knew about the Sleeper.

Chapter 32

Pi vs. Pie

"Big deal, you know about the Sleeper, and how we got through the wall of fog. Funny story, isn't it? Who is that guy, anyway?"

"A crazy old geezer who thinks he's the mystical gatekeeper for South Elysium. Lucky for me he sleeps most of the year."

"You're really not Mike the Mechanic?"

"What are you doing here? This is a highly restricted area. I could have you shot for being here."

"Wait, what? No, we're just trying to return something to Charon the Ferryman."

"Interesting. Care to tell me about it, little man?"

"Why would you call me that?"

"Because I'm over seven feet tall and you're barely touching four feet."

"I happen to be five feet nine inches tall, and there's no way you're seven feet tall. Six foot three, tops."

"What are you returning to Charon? Anything I should know about?"

"What do you do here, exactly? And why is there a

town filled with androids who don't know they're androids and never grow old?'

"You're a clever little boy, aren't you?"

Odo's fists were clenched, his knuckles white. This was the rudest, most annoying being he had ever had the misfortune to meet.

Sephie stepped up onto the boat, giving Bob the Mechanic a bright smile. "Hi, Bob, my name is Sephie Crumb."

Bob the Mechanic returned her smile. "Hi, Sephie, it's nice to meet you. I hope you're having an enjoyable visit here in South Elysium. Let me know if there's anything at all I can do to make your stay more pleasant. You're more than welcome to borrow my boat for as long as you'd like."

Odo was staring red hot burning daggers at Bob the Mechanic. What game was he playing? This was exactly what Mike the Mechanic had done. There's no way this wasn't Mike the Mechanic playing some twisted little trick.

Sephie gave a cheery smile. "Thank you so much, Bob, that's so kind of you. We really appreciate it."

Odo took a deep breath. "That really would be great, Bob. Thanks so much. We're kind of curious about South Elysium and those androids, though. Any chance you could tell us what that's all about?"

"I'd be happy to, right after you take my Three Question Challenge, little man. Are you up for it? You're not going to cry are you, because you look like you want to."

Odo cracked. "You're Mike the Mechanic and you know it! He gave us a ridiculous three question challenge, gave me insanely hard questions and gave Sephie an incredibly easy one."

"I'm truly sorry to hear that, Odo. I do my very best to keep all the questions at the same level of difficulty, no matter who is answering them."

Sephie said, "It sounds fun, I love taking tests. How many correct answers do we have to get?"

"Easy peasy, just get one correct answer and I'll tell you everything you want to know. Nothing to it. Who wants to go first?"

Odo gritted his teeth. "I'll go first, Mike."

"Bravo, young man. Well done. Let's start off with a math question. Are you pretty good at math? You seem like you would be."

"I've gotten an A in every math class I've ever taken."

"Impressive. You should do well then. I knew you'd be good at math. Okay, do you know what pi is?"

"That's easy, pi is the ratio of the circumference of any circle to the diameter of that circle. Regardless of the circle's size, the ratio will always equal pi. In decimal form, the value of pi is approximately 3.14."

"I'm impressed, you do know your math, sir."

"So I got it right?"

"Oh, sorry, that wasn't the question. Now, is pi a rational number or an irrational number?"

"Easy, it's an irrational number, meaning its decimal form never ends and never repeats."

"Again, I am stunned by your mathematical prowess. Very good, sir."

"I got the right answer?"

"Oh, sorry again, that wasn't the question. The question is, *what are the first ten thousand digits, in correct order, of the pi decimal?* You have thirty seconds to answer. Go!"

Odo thought his face was going to burst into flames. "What? That's impossible! Even if I knew all the numbers there's no way I could possibly list them all in–"

"Oh, time's up, I'm so sorry, bad luck indeed. Are you ready for your second question, or would you like a moment to gather your thoughts? I'll try to give you an easy one, no math at all since that doesn't appear to be your strong suit. The question will have a short, simple, one word answer. How does that sound?"

Odo shrugged. "Fine. Bring it on, *Mike.*"

"Great attitude, Odo, and that's really the secret to a happy life isn't it? Having a good positive attitude about everything, seeing the bright side, the glass is always half full?"

"Right, half full."

"Okay, here's the question. For the win, *what is my favorite kind of pie?* I'll repeat it for you, *what is my favorite kind of pie?* You have thirty seconds to answer. Go!"

"That's ridiculous, how am I supposed to know your favorite kind of pie? You're completely insane, and there's no way you're not Mike the–"

"Oopsy doops, bad luck again, I'm afraid, your time is up. The answer was *groozenberry*, My favorite kind of pie is *groozenberry pie*. Better luck next time. You've been a great contestant, Odo, and a good sport. Shall we let Sephie give it a shot? She seems like an exceptionally bright young lady. I love her orange hair, don't you? It's so cute, wouldn't you agree?"

Odo's face was carved from stone.

"Okay, Sephie Crumb, it's all up to you, everything is resting on your more than capable shoulders. Let me know when you're ready, and I'll give you the final question of Bob the Mechanic's Three Question Challenge Extravaganza. It's all or nothing, the final question."

"I'm ready, Bob."

"Okay, here we go. For the money, Sephie Crumb, *what is your favorite kind of pie*? I'll repeat it for you, *what is your favorite kind of pie?*"

"Oh, boy, that's a tough one, so many pies to choose from. I guess I'd have to say…um… apple. That's what I'm going with, my favorite kind of pie is apple."

Bob clapped his hands together. "Absolutely correct! Well done, Sephie Crumb, you did it! You beat the Three Question Challenge. Quite a feather in your cap, I'd say."

"Thanks, Bob. It was a toss up between apple and cherry, but I just somehow knew it was apple." She turned to Odo with a bright smile. "Wasn't that fun? I love taking tests."

Odo glared at Bob. "Now we get to ask you questions?"

Bob gave a cheery smile. "Ask away, my translucent young friend."

"Okay, what is this place? Where are we, exactly?"

Chapter 33

Q&A

Bob rubbed his chin, staring at Odo. "Where are you? That is your question?"

Odo nodded.

"You're in South Elysium on the Summerland River in a lovely wooden boat. How's that?"

Odo was about to say something very rude when Sephie interrupted, saying, "What is South Elysium exactly? And why do the androids have their own little village? And why isn't there a sun in the sky?"

"All excellent questions, Sephie. You are quite a perceptive young lady. It's complicated, but I'll do the best I can to explain it. First of all, the lack of a sun. You are not on a spherical world, you are on the Plane of Percupio, a flat, infinitely large plane stretching out in all directions forever and ever. So, no orbiting bodies to be found here, no stars and planets, just light from above which comes and goes in a precise mathematical rhythmic pattern. Quite different from the dimensions you are used to."

Emmy raised her hand. "Bob, are there lots of different little towns and villages all over South Elysium?"

Bob eyed Emmy. "Well, Emmy, if you were to fly up into the sky and get a bird's eye view of Percupio, you would see an infinite number of towns and villages from every era and every world and every universe scattered across a never-ending plane. As you may have guessed, South Elysium is one infinitesimally small piece of the Plane of Percupio."

Emmy's eyes narrowed slightly. Why had he mentioned flying up in the air and getting a bird's eye view? Had he seen her? Was he reading her thoughts? Did he know she could fly?

Silas said, "What about the androids? How did everyone get here, and why are they here? Are they all dead?"

"Excellent questions. Almost everyone on the Plane of Percupio has died on their world, but they are not yet in the Land of the Dead. The Plane of Percupio, in very simplistic terms, is the Land of the Almost Dead."

Odo said, "Why aren't they in the Land of the Dead?"

"Let's say you failed a required math class because you didn't know the first ten thousand decimals of pi, and you couldn't graduate. What would happen?"

"I'd have to take the class again. Maybe in summer school?"

"Precisely. The Plane of Percupio is summer school for every life form in existence from every time in existence, although time, as you may be aware, doesn't actually exist."

"What classes are they taking?"

"An infinite variety of classes, tailor made for each individual, sometimes simply being granted lifelong desires which they believed would bring them happiness, teaching them about the true nature of happiness. Just as an aside, the source of true happiness is not a big pile of gold coins."

Odo glared at him. "I already know that, Mike. Are you talking about people who always wanted to be rich or famous?"

"Exactly, anything they thought would make them happy, but really wouldn't. There are no physical objects in existence that can bring true happiness, and that includes a big chest of shiny gold coins."

Odo gritted his teeth. "Right. So what about the androids?"

"They live in a town where nothing changes, no one grows old, no one grows up, no one gets sick, and no one dies. Their bodies are indestructible creations of a highly advanced nature. The red button shuts them off, in the rare event that repairs become necessary."

"But they don't know they're in android bodies?"

"Correct, they are simply experiencing what they thought would make them happy on their world. When they realize that happiness comes from understanding the perfection of change, they move on to the Land of the Dead."

Emmy raised her hand again. "If the Plane of Percupio is infinitely big, how come we don't see billions of people heading to the River Styx to cross over?"

"A marvelous question, and one with a simple answer. The Land of the Dead is a house with many doors. And by many, I mean an infinite number."

"So you don't have to take Charon's ferry across the River Styx to get there?"

"Charon built his ferry several thousand years ago, hoping to turn it into a thriving enterprise. It was for a while, but times have changed, and Charon has not. There are some people from certain eras who take his ferry, mostly for sentimental reasons, so they can say they crossed the River Styx on Charon's Ferry, but the numbers dwindle as time marches on. Not that time actually marches, or even exists."

Emmy said, "Is it true that Charon can bring someone back from the Land of the Dead?"

Bob the Mechanic took a seat on the bench next to Emmy.

"You are referring to your brother Jacob?"

"How did you know that?"

"I'm Bob the Mechanic, I know lots of things. You have Charon's lost Key Spike, the one stolen by Odysseus?"

"We do. Someone said if we return it, he'll let us bring one person back from the Land of the Dead."

"Quite true. And you wish to bring your brother back? You are certain this is what you want?"

"What will happen if Jacob comes back? How does it work?"

"It is very complicated, sometimes bringing with it certain unforeseen changes."

Odo raised his hand. "I have a real quick question, *Mike*. How come you're so nice to everyone else, but so mean to me? And who are you, really? Are you Mike the Mechanic?"

"You need to be challenged, Odo Whitley of 11949 Asper Street, Bedford Falls. You need to discover on your own who and what you are. All four of you have been brought together for a reason, part of a very complex and ancient tapestry."

Emmy said, "I'm part of it?"

"Indeed you are, young lady. I will add that you have passed many difficult trials in your life with flying colors."

Emmy was silent. Flying colors? He had emphasized the word flying. He definitely knew she could fly, but he wasn't telling the others. That was interesting.

Odo said, "You're not Mike the Mechanic?"

"Oh good heavens, you just can't let anything go, can you?"

"I was just curious."

"Which is one of your most admirable traits, and the reason you find yourself on such an extraordinary adventure with your three friends. To answer your question, I am Bob the Mechanic. I am also Mike the Mechanic. I exist simultaneously in ten thousand thousand different planes of existence with ten thousand thousand different names, but my job is the same in every world. I fix leaky dihydrogen monoxide pipes."

Odo snapped. "You're doing it again! I know what dihydrogen monoxide is, Mike. It's water, H2O, two atoms of hydrogen and one atom of oxygen. You're saying all you do is fix leaky water pipes? That you're a plumber? That's ridiculous, and you know it!"

"Did you know the veins on your forehead bulge out when you get angry?"

Sephie nodded. "It's true, I've noticed that."

Odo glared at her.

Bob the Mechanic stood up. "Time to go, I'm afraid. Old Mr. Groozenberry in apartment 2B has a leaky dihydrogen monoxide pipe that needs fixing."

Odo could feel his face burning. "There's no Mr. Groozenberry, you're just making that up! That's the kind of pie you said was your favorite–"

There was a flash of blue light and Bob the Mechanic was gone.

Silas leaned back in his seat, his eyes on Emmy. "We're on the infinite Plane of Percupio. How crazy is that?"

Odo muttered, "Something is seriously wrong with that guy."

Chapter 34

Paradise Falls

"Push us off!"

Silas untied the boat, using an oar to push them away from the dock. "I'll row us out into the current."

Odo flopped down onto the deck, staring up at the green rippling sky. "What do you think is up there if there aren't any stars or planets?"

"Nothing, I guess. What I don't get is how Percupio could go on forever in all directions. It doesn't seem possible."

"I don't get why Bob the Mechanic gave me the crazy hard questions and you get ridiculously easy ones."

"I know why, but I'm not going to tell you. You have to figure it out for yourself."

"He said I needed to be challenged. Probably because I'm so smart."

"Wrong."

"What do you mean, wrong?"

"That's what he told you, but it wasn't the real answer. He was tricking you again."

Odo gave her a dark look, his gaze once again on the green rippling sky. "There must be something up there, it can't just be nothing."

Sephie smiled.

"What's so funny?"

"You are, Odo Whitley. You're funny, but it's the best kind of funny there is."

Silas stood up, looking down the river, tilting his head. "Do you hear that? That roaring sound?"

Emmy said, "I hear it. What is it?"

Odo cried out, "Waterfall! It's a waterfall! I can see the mist coming up from below the falls!" He grabbed the oars. "We have to get to shore!"

Silas grabbed the second set of oars, the two friends rowing frantically, the roar of the falls growing louder as the current pulled them down the river.

"Row harder! I can see the edge of the waterfall!"

The good news was they reached the shore, the bad news was the current was much stronger there, the boat thudding and crashing against the rocks as it was dragged toward the falls.

There was a flash of blue light, a steel grappling hook appearing in Sephie's hands. She tied it to the mooring line, swung it around in a wide circle and let it loose, the heavy hook landing in the dense forest undergrowth.

"Hold on!"

The line jerked tight, Odo almost tumbling out of the

boat when it came to a shuddering halt, still rocking wildly in the powerful current. The boat lurched forward a few feet, then stopped again.

"Get off before the grappling hook pulls out!"

The four companions leaped from the wildly rocking boat onto the shore, Odo tumbling into a thorny bush. "Ow! Why do I always land in these stupid thorns?"

There was a tearing noise as the steel hook pulled the bushes out of the ground, ripping past Odo, missing him by a few inches. Moments later the boat was gone, disappearing over the falls.

Odo got to his feet, staring at the raging river. "That was way too close."

Emmy turned to Sephie. "You saved our lives. If you hadn't made that grappling hook, we would have…" She didn't finish her sentence.

Odo's eyes were still on the roaring falls.

Silas said, "That was so close. There should have been warning signs posted along the riverbank."

Odo nodded. "Bob the Mechanic never mentioned the falls. He let us have the boat and didn't tell us about them. He had to have known how dangerous it was."

"Maybe he's like Wikerus, not allowed to alter certain timelines, letting events take their natural course."

"You mean like us going over the falls and getting smashed to pieces on the rocks below? Events like that?"

"Are you dead, Odo Whitley?"

"That's not the point, he should have told us about–"

"Are you dead? Did you go over the falls?"

"No."

"Maybe he knew we'd be okay."

Odo looked dubious. "Maybe, or maybe not. I don't trust that guy, he has some serious issues."

"What do we do now?"

Emmy pointed through the trees to a white sign with black painted letters nailed to a branch.

Welcome to Paradise Falls
Population 2

They wove their way through the woods, Silas studying the sign. "Only two people live here? That's kind of weird."

"This whole place is weird, people living in little towns on some infinite plane and not knowing where they really are or what they're doing there? How crazy is that?"

Silas shrugged. "It's not much different than living on a giant ball of rock floating in space in an infinitely vast universe."

Odo nodded. "That's true. I hadn't thought of that."

"Let's hike down to the base of the falls and look for a boat."

Sephie took Odo's hand. "Welcome to Paradise Falls, Odo Whitley."

The friends hiked through the trees, a small town coming into view. "That's a lot of houses for a town with only two people."

Emmy said, "Let's check it out, see who lives here."

Odo gave a yelp, stumbling backwards. "Gahh! What is that?" He pointed to an eight-inch long fat green centipede slithering through the grass. "That's disgusting. I hate centipedes."

Silas called out, "There's two more! They're all over."

Odo said, "Forget this town, I don't even want to know who lives here. Probably two giant alien centipedes."

"Maybe they only live in the forest."

The friends walked down the main street, Odo keeping a wary eye out for creepy green centipedes.

"I guess this is the town center. There's no stores though, which is strange. They should at least have a general store."

Emmy said, "That's a gift shop over there. I should get a souvenir to bring back, maybe a mug or a tee shirt."

"*I heart Paradise Falls?*"

Silas laughed. "How about, *Odo went to the Plane of Percupio and all I got was this lousy tee shirt.*"

"You laugh, but they could have really cool stuff here." Emmy pushed open the door, entering the shop.

Odo stepped in after her, looking around, a puzzled expression on his face. "I don't get it, all the gifts are wrapped. How do you know what you're getting?"

"Maybe they're surprise gifts?"

"There are no prices on them and no one to pay. I don't see a cash register."

"Maybe they're free."

"And maybe two giant green alien centipedes are watching us on hidden cameras, waiting to see if we steal anything so they can jump out and eat us."

Sephie stared at Odo. "Something is wrong with your brain, Odo Whitley."

Emmy laughed, "I think he's funny."

Silas grabbed a colorfully wrapped gift from a table, shaking it. "Can't tell what it is, but like I always say, there's only one way to find out. Here goes." He ripped the paper off, revealing a shiny white cardboard box. "Looks expensive."

When Silas pulled the lid off the box he saw the very last thing he was expecting to see. He screamed, the box tumbling to the floor.

Chapter 35

The Gift Shop

Odo skittered backwards when he saw the six green centipedes spill out of the box and race across the floor, disappearing through a small hole in the wall.

His look of curiosity had transformed to one of horror. "Time to go! I officially hate Paradise Falls, I do not want to know who lives here, and I'm never coming back."

Silas said, "Agreed. Let's go."

Sephie studied the piles of unopened gifts. "Does anyone else think it's incredibly strange that a gift shop would have beautifully wrapped packages filled with creepy green centipedes?"

Odo said, "Gosh, Sephie, what could possibly be strange about five hundred gift boxes filled with green centipedes?"

They exited the store, Emmy motioning for them to stop, pointing to one of the houses. "Look over there."

Silas eyed the small house with the white picket

fence and lovely rose garden, a man and a woman sitting on the front porch. "Those must be the two residents of Paradise Falls."

Odo said, "Let's go talk to them. I want to see if they know anything about the gift shop. I changed my mind, I want to know why there are centipedes in the boxes. It will drive me insane if I don't find out."

Sephie grinned. She knew exactly why Bob the Mechanic gave Odo such impossibly hard questions, and she also knew what he was trying to teach him.

Odo approached the house, giving a friendly wave. "Hi!"

The man gave a slight nod, the woman did not.

Odo said, "Do you guys know anything about the gift shop?

"Good place to go if you're running low on centipedes."

"Why are there centipedes in the boxes? Who put them there?"

The man shrugged. "Dunno."

"Have you lived here long?"

"Not sure, been a while though."

"You opened some of the gifts in the store?"

"Lots of them. Nothing but those blasted green centipedes."

The woman nodded. "I must have opened fifty of them. All centipedes. Don't even bother anymore."

"Who lives in the other houses?"

"All gone, moved out, one by one. Just us now."

The woman said, "Where are you folks–"

The man snapped at her, "Mind your own business. Nothing good will come of it."

Odo blinked. What was that about?

Sephie said, "We should go now, it was nice talking to you."

The man nodded.

As they walked away, Odo whispered, "How weird was that?"

Sephie grabbed Odo's hand. "We have to go back to the gift shop. Now."

"Did you want to pick up a few boxes of centipedes for your mom?"

"I'm being pulled there. It's important, Odo Whitley, like when I found the ticket to Plindor in the antique store. Some invisible force was pulling me there. We have to go back."

"Okay, let's go."

The four friends stepped back into the shop. Silas strolled over to a table, picking up a package and handing it to Odo with an enormous grin. "Happy birthday, Odo. I got this just for you. It's a big surprise, and I really hope you like it. It took me a long time to find just the right present for you, one I knew you would cherish forever."

Odo gave an equally cheesy grin, shaking the box. "Thanks, Silas, that's so thoughtful of you. Hmm... it's hard to tell what it is, but it sounds like it might be green and have lots of legs."

"Go ahead and open it, unless you're chicken. Bawk bawk baaawk!"

212

Odo rolled his eyes. "Nothing scares the incredible Translucent Boy." He ripped off the wrapping paper, setting the box on a table, gently lifting the lid. Silas was grinning like a madman.

Odo peered into the box. "No way."

"What is it?"

Odo reached in and pulled out a gleaming red smart phone. "This is amazing, super expensive." He flipped it over, looking at the back of it, his eyes widening.

"What?"

"It's engraved." He held it up for the others to see.

Best wishes to Odo from his old friend Silas

Silas' jaw dropped. "Just when I thought things couldn't get any stranger. That is so impossible."

Sephie said, "I think I know what's happening."

"What?"

She picked up a gift, handing it to Emmy. "This is for you, Emmy, for being such a good friend."

Emmy unwrapped the box, setting it down on the table, slowly raising the lid. "Wow!" She pulled out a beautiful gold bracelet inlaid with small sparkling emeralds. "It's so beautiful, thank you so much."

"Is it engraved?"

Emmy studied the inside of the band.

For my dear friend Emmy, from Sephie.

The four friends stared silently at the phone and the

sparkling gold bracelet.

Odo broke the silence. "It's a gift shop. You have to give it to someone as a gift, you can't open it yourself." He picked up a box, handing it to Sephie. "This is for you, Sephie Crumb, my best friend in the world."

Sephie opened it, pulling out a heart shaped gold locket on a delicate gold chain, a single diamond in the center of the heart. "It's beautiful, Odo."

Silas said, "Is it engraved?"

"I don't see anything."

"Open the locket, maybe it says something inside."

Sephie opened it, read it, then closed it.

"What does it say?"

"Um... it says...just some stuff. Emmy, you should give something to Silas."

Emmy grabbed a box, handing it to Silas. "This is for you, Silas Ward. I'm glad you sat next to me on the bus."

"So am I." Silas grinned, opening the box. "Whoa, check out this watch! It's incredible, super nice."

Sephie smiled. "Is it engraved, Silas? What does it say? Would you like to read it out loud to us?"

Silas flipped it over, reading the small letters on the back, his face turning bright red.

"What does it say?"

"Just some stuff. We should go."

Sephie laughed, grabbing two more packages. "Not yet, we have some unfinished business to attend to." She exited the shop, heading back to the man and the woman sitting on the porch.

The man's eyes were on the gifts in Sephie's hands.

"Get those things away from us."

"You have to trust me. I promise you won't regret it."

The man gave her a suspicious look. "What do we have to do?"

Sephie handed one of the gifts to him and one to the woman. "Don't open them now, but after we go, I want you to say something nice about each other, then exchange these gifts. Something very good will happen, I promise."

The woman whispered, "Are you an angel?"

Sephie shook her head. "No. Wait until we leave, then give each other your gift."

"We will."

The friends headed back into the forest, Odo spotting a sign next to a narrow trail.

This way to the base
of Paradise Falls

"That's it, we follow this trail down to the river."

"What do you think will happen when they give each other the gifts?"

"I'm not sure, but I think it will be something very good."

Twenty minutes later they arrived at the bottom of the falls, Odo gazing up at the tons of water thundering three hundred feet down into the broad Summerland River, the air filled with a soft cool mist. "That's incredible! Look at all that water!"

"Odo! Look!"

"What is it?" He spun around, his eyes on Sephie. She pointed to a wooden sign next to the trailhead.

Welcome to Paradise Falls
Population 0

Before Odo could say anything, the sign vanished.

Chapter 36

Tunnels

"You think they passed their test, moved on to the Land of the Dead?"

"I think so, Odo Whitley."

"So the lesson is, it's better to give than to receive? Unless it's a super cool red smart phone, then it's way better to get one."

"Not funny, Odo."

Emmy said, "There's another saying, a more important one. *It's not the gift, it's the thought that counts.*" She glanced over at Silas.

Sephie touched the gold locket hanging around her neck. "You're right, Emmy, it's the thought behind the gift that really counts."

Odo was afraid to ask what was engraved on the locket he'd given to Sephie. He hoped it was something nice, but not too embarrassing, not all weird and mushy.

"So we hike along the river until we find a boat?"

"I guess so. Maybe we'll run into a little town."

"Great, another crazy Percupio village."

Odo rubbed his hands together. "Maybe we'll run

into a town full of people who always wanted to be super rich and they all live in giant mansions and they'll give us free bags of gold coins."

"Focus, Odo Whitley. Don't forget what Bob the Mechanic said about gold coins and happiness."

"I know they don't bring happiness, I just want to have a bunch of them so I can buy cool stuff."

The group of friends hiked downriver for over six hours without finding a town or a boat. Odo sat down on a fallen tree trunk. "Do we even know how much farther it is to the River Styx?"

"The blacksmith said it was three hundred and nine miles."

"So we have about a mile left?"

"Not even close."

"We need to find a boat. Or maybe a futuristic high tech town that has anti-grav cars."

"Less talking, more walking." Sephie grinned, nudging Emmy.

Odo staggered to his feet. "So tired."

"You're not tired, you're just bored. Get moving."

"All these trees look the same."

An hour later, as they were heading up a steep hill, Silas motioned for them to stop. "Do you hear that?"

"It's a clinking sound, like someone hitting stone."

Odo headed up the hill. "Maybe it's super rich people counting their gold coins."

Four jaws dropped when they crested the hill.

"What is that?"

"A giant black wall?"

"It must be five hundred feet tall."

"And it goes in both directions as far as I can see."

Odo kicked at the ground. "Why would they have a stupid giant wall here? What's wrong with this place? How are we supposed to get past it?"

"That clinking sound is coming from the wall."

"Let's go see what it is."

"Probably giant death lizards sharpening their claws."

The four friends made their way down the hill, hiking through the forest, arriving at the megalithic black structure.

Odo said, "That explains the clinking sound." He pointed to a long row of people sitting at the base of the wall, chipping at it with small metal hammers.

"What are they doing?"

"I think they're trying to tunnel through it, get to the other side."

"They've hardly even made a dent in it. It looks super hard, like obsidian or something."

Silas said, "None of them are even close to making a tunnel. They've chipped off maybe an inch or two at the most."

"Stay here, I'm going to go talk to that guy." Odo walked over to a man wearing a ragged gray cloak, his eyes half closed as he chipped at the wall with his little hammer.

"How's it going?"

The man didn't seem to notice him.

"How long have you been chipping at the wall?"

"Get away from me. Get your own hammer."

Odo stepped away from the man. "Sorry, I wasn't trying to take your hammer, I was just wondering how long it takes to tunnel through the wall. We're trying to get to the River Styx."

The man gave a harsh laugh. "Good luck with that."

"Right. How long have you been at it?"

"Don't know. A long time, maybe even longer. Maybe forever."

"Hasn't someone already made a tunnel you can go through?"

"If you stop chipping, the wall grows back and you lose everything."

"The wall grows back?"

"You heard me."

"Okay, thanks."

Odo ran back to the others.

"What did he say?"

"It's great news, he's been there forever and the wall grows back if you stop chipping at it."

"That doesn't sound like great news."

Odo looked up at the wall. "Anyone have a five hundred foot tall ladder I can borrow?"

"There has to be a way past it. The wall has to end somewhere. We can go around it."

"I don't think it ends. I think it goes on forever across Percupio."

"I know what to do. Sephie, stand on my shoulders and see if you can climb over it."

"Maybe if we all chipped at it together?"

"That guy has been chipping at it maybe forever and he's gotten nowhere. Wait, can you shape us a helicopter?"

"That's way too big, Odo Whitley. "

Emmy said nothing, studying the wall. She knew she could fly over it, but the Sinarian had made her promise not to tell the others she could fly. If she broke her promise they would take away her power. What she didn't understand is why they would give her this power but not let her use it.

"So what are we going to do?"

"Silas, run into the wall as fast as you can and see if you can knock it over."

"Wait, even better, we could use your head for a battering ram."

Sephie burst out laughing. "Good one."

Odo laughed. "Okay, that was pretty funny."

"There has to be some way through it."

Odo slapped his forehead. "What was I thinking? I can make a translucent doorway! I can let everyone through."

He darted down to the wall, placing his hand on it. Five minutes later he came back, shaking his head. "It's not working. It's not an ordinary wall. It's something very different."

Odo watched the long row of people chipping at the wall with their little steel hammers. "You'd think they'd all get together and come up with some cool idea, like a hot air balloon or a giant wooden ladder or something."

"Can you shape a hot air balloon?"

"I can't shape big things like that. There's a limit, just like there's a limit to how much you can lift."

"There's a billion trees here, we could cut them down and make scaffolding and climb over it."

"It's five hundred feet tall, Odo."

Odo sat down, leaning back against a tree. "We're doomed. There's no way through. We have to go home."

Emmy slumped down onto the grass, looking up at the wall.

Chapter 37

Emmy's Plan

Emmy waited until the others were sleeping. They had agreed to stay another day or two, to think about it, try to come up with a plan to get past the wall.

"I don't have to tell them I can fly. I'll take the spike, fly over the wall and bring it to Charon. It won't take me long to fly there, it's only a few hundred miles."

She crept over to where Odo was sleeping, reaching gingerly into his backpack, pulling the Key Spike out.

"Got it. Now it's up and over the wall and off to see Charon the Ferryman."

She raised her arms, transforming her body, her legs straight, a glorious feeling of freedom flowing through her. She floated up off the ground, flying toward the wall. "I wish they could see this. I wish Silas could see this."

She soared straight up, listing to the clinking sound of a hundred hammers chipping at the wall. "Those poor people. Maybe I can fly them over the wall."

She was precisely four hundred and fifty-nine feet in the air when something very unexpected happened. The wall shot up another hundred feet.

"What? That's not possible, there's no way that can happen."

It happened again when she was five hundred and fifty-nine feet in the air.

She gave up at one thousand, seven hundred and fifty-nine feet, a horrible sick feeling rolling through her. She wanted to cry and never stop. She couldn't bring Jacob back, even with her amazing power.

She flew back, landing silently, slipping the spike into Odo's pack. She crawled into her sleeping bag, closing her eyes. She couldn't even tell them she'd tried, couldn't tell them there was no way over the wall, and most likely no way under it. Jacob might not be coming home after all.

Odo and Sephie were the first ones up.

"Let's go check out the wall, maybe we'll think of something. I wonder if we could tunnel under it?"

"I don't think it's that simple, but I think there is an answer. Bob the Mechanic said Percupio is the Land of the Almost Dead, that everyone here has to learn some life lesson before they can move on."

"Right. How does that help us?"

"It means the solution has something to do with people learning a lesson."

"Like don't visit Percupio because of all the lessons you have to learn?"

"No, Odo Whitley, not like that at all."

They reached the wall, Odo running his hand across it. "It didn't react at all when I tried to create a doorway. It might not even be a physical wall." He gave a sigh, leaning back against the gleaming monolithic structure, looking straight up. "Who built this dumb thing anyway?"

Sephie gave him an odd smile, her hand on the gold heart shaped pendant he'd given her. She moved closer to him. "Aren't you curious at all about the inscription on the pendant you gave me?"

Odo froze. "Um... it says something nice about you?"

She nodded. "Don't you want to know exactly what it says about me?"

Odo could feel his face turning red. "It's not super embarrassing is it?"

"Not to me."

"Do I really want to see it?"

Sephie said, "I want you to see it, because I know you meant it." She reached out and took Odo's hand in hers.

"It says–"

A most extraordinary thing happened before Sephie could finish her sentence, before she could tell Odo what the inscription said. The two friends tumbled backwards through the wall into a dense thicket of tall green grass.

Odo gave a screech, jumping up. "What happened? Did we go through the wall? Are we on the other side?"

"We fell right through it, like it wasn't even there."

"How? What did we do? How do we get back and tell the others?" Odo pushed his hand against the wall.

"It's solid. There's no way they can hear us if we yell. They won't know what happened to us. They'll think we went home. They'll never know what–"

"Stop, you need to focus. Let's think about it. We can figure it out. Okay, you were leaning against the wall, and I was about to tell you what the locket said."

"But you didn't tell me, we just fell through onto the grass."

A smile appeared on Sephie's face. "I think I know how to get through the wall, Odo Whitley."

"How do we get through?"

"I'll tell you if you read the inscription on the locket."

Odo frowned. "What?"

"I'll tell you if you read the inscription."

"Do I have to read it out loud?"

"No." She handed him the locket. He looked at her, then gingerly opened it, reading it silently. "Whoa." He raised his eyebrows.

"Whoa, indeed, Odo Whitley."

He closed it, dropping it into her hand. "Okay, so, um… how do we get through the wall?"

Sephie studied his brainwaves. "You're not embarrassed."

Odo shook his head. "I thought I would be, but I'm not."

"I'm glad. Now, back to business. What's the last thing that happened before we fell through the wall?"

"You grabbed my hand."

"Bingo."

"You can't say bingo, you said it's totally annoying."

"It's only annoying when you say it, not when I say it."

"That's even more annoying. Wait, we fell through the wall because we were holding hands? That makes no sense."

"It makes a lot of sense in Percupio. What did all the people chipping at the wall have in common?"

"They had hammers, they were sitting, they'd been there a really long time... and they were alone. They weren't helping each other, they were each making their own tunnel."

"Bingo again. One of the first things you said when you saw them was, why don't they all work together and figure out a way through the wall, build a ladder or a hot air balloon?"

"They don't want to ask for help. Maybe they're afraid to, or they don't trust other people, or they think it makes them look weak, or people won't want to help them, or they won't like them because they asked for help."

"Probably all of those things." Sephie took Odo's hand, the two friends walking back through the wall.

They raced up the hill, Odo running over to Silas' sleeping bag, kicking his leg.

"Wakey, wakey, little Silas! Guess where we've been?"

Silas rolled over. "Five minutes, Mom."

"We know how to get through the wall!"

Chapter 38

Lead a Horse to Water

"You just hold hands and walk through?"

"Watch this." Odo took Sephie's hand, moving his other arm through the wall. "It's like it's not even there, a spectral wall."

"That's amazing. So they just want people to ask for help?"

"It's more than that. They want people to trust each other, to help each other, not be afraid of looking weak, to understand that everyone needs help sometimes, and to understand that most people really do like helping other people."

"If it wasn't for you guys I'd probably still be hiding under a blanket, terrified of ghosts. Oh, I thought up another good name for us. It's really cool."

"What is it?"

"*Ghostwatcher's Warriors.*"

"We're not warriors, but if we were, we'd be *The Translucent Boy's Band of Warriors.*"

228

"That makes it sound like we're a boy band, like we sing and dance, a boy band made up of singing warriors."

"It doesn't sound like that at all."

Emmy said, "It kind of does, plus it would be confusing to have two girls in a boy band, and only have two boys in it. Most boy bands have at least five or six boys and no girls. That's why they call them boy bands."

Odo could feel his neck getting hot. "It's not a boy band, it's the *Translucent Boy's Band of Warriors.*"

"It doesn't work, it sounds like you're saying it's a boy band, and the Translucent Boy is the lead singer. Do you know how to sing? Can you dance at all?"

Sephie was gaping at them. "Are you done? Have you forgotten why we're here?"

"It doesn't matter what it sounds like because we're not warriors. But just to be clear, it didn't sound like we were a boy band."

Silas said, "We should tell everyone how to get through the wall. It might force them to make friends."

"Good idea. I'll go tell that guy." Odo strolled over to the man in the ragged gray cloak, watching him chip at the wall with his hammer. "How's it going?"

The man gave him a dark look.

"In case you're interested, we figured out how to get through the wall."

"I already know how to get through it. What do you think I'm doing?"

"There's an easy way to get through it, though. Give

me your hand and I'll show you."

"Back off or you'll be worm food. You're not getting my hammer. Go find your own."

"Right, it's just that if you hold hands with someone, you can walk right through the wall like it's not there."

The man glared at Odo, still chipping at the wall. "Did someone drop a rock on your head?"

"It's true. It's also true that you're here to learn that it's okay to ask for help."

"Take your crazy somewhere else, friend. I don't have time for this. Take a long hike off a short dock."

Odo walked back to the others. "It didn't go as well as I had planned."

"He thinks you're crazy?"

"Correct."

Emmy said, "Let's show him instead of telling him. Come on." She grabbed Silas' hand and they walked over to the gray cloaked man.

"What do you want? You got another box of crazy for me?"

"Watch what happens when I'm holding her hand." Silas moved his arm through the wall, then pulled it back out. "See, it really works. If you hold hands with someone you can walk right through."

Fear rippled across the man's face. "Dark magic! Get away from me, demon!" He screamed out, "DEMONS! KILL THE DEMONS!"

"Okay, time to go." Silas and Emmy stepped through the wall. A moment later they were joined by Odo and Sephie.

Emmy said, "What did we learn from that, class?"

"You can lead a horse to water, but you can't make it walk through a wall?"

Emmy laughed. "Almost, but not quite."

Sephie wasn't smiling. "I feel so sorry for them."

"We did the best we could. We showed them how to get through"

"I know, it's still sad though. They just can't see it, even when it's right in front of them."

Odo headed toward the river. "Keep an eye open for boats. Or ice cream shops that specialize in extra large salted caramel banana splits."

Sephie gave Odo a sideways glance, a smile flickering across her face. He was so funny.

An hour later the black wall was behind them, the four adventurers strolling along the banks of the Summerland River.

"I hope we can find a boat. It's a lot faster than going through all the forests and underbrush. I've been stabbed by thorns at least five hundred times."

They spun around when they heard the shrill blast of a steam whistle.

Odo's mouth was hanging open. "Whoa, I was seriously not expecting that."

"It's a steamboat, a stern wheeler like they used to have on the Mississippi River!"

"What's it doing here?"

The huge vessel was chugging down the river toward them, the steam whistle blasting again, the ship's massive paddle churning up the water.

"It's so loud!"

"It's slowing down! I can see its name! It's called the *Elysium Belle*."

The gigantic rotating paddle wheel slowed down, then reversed, fighting the current, holding the boat stationary in the river. A man wearing a blue coat with brass buttons stepped out of the pilot house, waving his hat at them. He picked up a megaphone, hollering, "Are you folks bound for the Land of the Dead?"

Odo yelled back, "We're headed for the River Styx!"

"All aboard then! We make a stop there before crossing over to the Land of the Dead."

"How much for a ticket?"

"No charge, sir! I'm contracted by the South Elysium Department of Transportation to carry passengers to the Land of the Dead."

Odo looked at the others. "What do you think? Want to ride on a cool steamboat?"

Emmy was practically jumping up and down. "Yes! How amazing would that be?"

Odo waved to the man in the blue suit. "We'll go!"

The man blew a silver whistle, two men in white uniforms lowering a wooden walkway onto the shore.

"All aboard the *Elysium Belle*!"

Chapter 39

The Elysium Belle

The four friends darted up the ramp onto the main deck of the steamboat.

"How cool is this? It's like we went back in time."

Odo nodded. "Plus, we don't have to row, and it's free."

One of the men in white pointed to a set of stairs. "Head on up to the boiler deck, visit the saloon."

They ran up the stairs, Odo stopping when he heard the old time piano music. "This is just like in the movies! Let's check it out." He pushed through the swinging doors, stepping into a crowded smoke-filled saloon, the walls lined with mirrors and red velvet embossed wallpaper.

Emmy's jaw dropped. "That guy looks like a Spanish conquistador."

Silas added, "And the guy he's playing cards with has four arms. And he's blue."

Emmy couldn't take her eyes off him. "Is he an alien?"

Odo nodded. "I think he's from Praelium."

"I'm looking at an alien, a blue alien with four

arms."

One of the card players, a tall man dressed like a gunslinger from the old west, jumped to his feet, knocking his chair back.

"I seen what you done, you four-armed cheatin' scoundrel! Eat lead, lizard face!" He yanked a heavy six-shooter from his holster, firing it three times at the blue alien, the roar of the gun deafening, smoke and fire shooting out of the barrel. He twirled the gun, flipping it smoothly back into his holster.

The blue alien hadn't moved, his eyes still on the gunslinger. "I'm already dead, moron, and cheating is part of the game. Sit down and play cards or I'll call the Captain and have him throw you into the river. Good luck getting to the Land of the Dead, cow person."

The gunslinger glared at him, slumping back down into his chair, flipping his cards over. "Six aces. I win, you scaly mutant."

The conquistador pulled out a long silver dagger, stabbing it into the wooden table. "There's no need for language like that, sir."

"What are you gonna do, stab me? We're all dead, ain't nobody gonna be killin' nobody. Don't it get hot wearin' that tin hat?"

The blue alien laughed. "You used a double negative, cow person."

The cowboy drew his six-shooter, setting it on the table in front of him, his eyes narrow slits. "Triple negative, lizard face. Better clean the wax outta them ears. If them wiggly things is ears."

The blue alien shrugged, setting his cards down. "Two full houses and a pair of jacks."

"You got twelve cards and we're playin' five card draw, you slitherin' snake!"

"You had six aces. Who's the cheatin' scoundrel now, cow person?"

Odo was waiting for the gunslinger to grab his six-gun when Sephie said, "Let's go watch the piano player."

"Okay." They pushed their way through the crowd, Odo almost knocking over a two-foot tall alien resembling a white chipmunk in a silver jump suit, a tall green drink in his hand. "Sorry!"

The alien shrugged. "It's all good, friend, and the drinks are free."

"You're on your way to the Land of the Dead?"

"Haven't decided yet. Lots of stuff to do in Percupio. I might stay here for a while, maybe do a little sightseeing, learn a few lessons."

"Sounds fun."

Odo and Sephie headed over to the piano player, Odo jumping out of the way as a massive furry black beast holding a short sword crashed into a table, his huge hand gripping the throat of a six-foot tall praying mantis.

"Try that again and they'll have to glue you back together, bug face."

"Really? Bug face is the best you can do?" There was a blur of motion, the praying mantis kicking the furry creature halfway across the room.

Sephie grabbed Odo's arm, pulling him over to the piano.

The piano player was straight out of an old western movie; black pants, a white shirt, black bow tie, and a red striped velvet vest. He was also a silver robot with eight fingers on each hand.

Sephie said, "You're amazing, where did you learn to play like that?"

The robot studied their faces, his eyes blinking rapidly. "I studied at the Juilliard School of Music for five years."

"You're kidding, the Juilliard School of Music?"

"Of course I'm kidding. You Earth guys are so gullible. First time in Percupio?"

"Yes, we're on our way to the River Styx to see Charon."

"You're dead?"

"We're not dead. Why does everyone keep asking us that?"

"Why do you want to see a sad case like Charon?"

"Why is he a sad case?"

"He's still ferrying people in a rickety two thousand year old wooden boat. No food, no entertainment. You couldn't even fit half a piano in that thing. The *Elysium Belle* is taking all his business. He won't last another year. That crazy old coot is finished."

"That's kind of sad, he's been ferrying people for such a long time."

"You have to keep up with the times. That's why the South Elysium Department of Transportation contracted the *Elysium Belle* to carry passengers. It's got every-thing, puts Charon's little rowboat to shame."

Odo blinked. "I just thought of something. How did the *Elysium Belle* get past the big black wall?"

"What big black wall?"

"About ten miles back, near Paradise Falls. And how did you get over the giant waterfall?"

We go up and down the Summerland River twice a week. Never seen a black wall or a waterfall, never heard of Paradise Falls. Of course, this is Percupio, so you never know."

"Right."

"Is everyone in Percupio here to learn life lessons?"

"Only if they want to. The paperwork is a nightmare for most of the lesson towns. You have to give them permission to block your memories for as long as you're there. Some folks don't want that. Lots of people just get reborn on their world instead of staying here."

"They get reborn?"

"If they want. Some folks do, some folks don't."

Sephie said, "Where are you from?"

"A little world called Plindor. Built and programmed there."

Odo gave a yelp. "No way! We've been to Plindor! We got kidnapped by pirates there, held prisoner on a landsailer called the *Canthus.*"

"No kidding? Small universe. I was built before the war, no landsailers and pirates then, but I've heard lots of stories. You were lucky to make it out alive."

Odo whispered, "Sephie is a Fortisian."

"The orange hair kind of gave it away, kiddo."

Odo ducked when a bottle flew past his head, smashing against the wall behind him.

"I better get back to playing, music seems to calm them down, not so many fights. My name is B9, by the way."

"I'm Odo and this is my friend Sephie. We should go find our friends. It was nice meeting you."

B9 nodded, swiveling around on the piano stool, hammering out a lively old Stephen Foster tune.

Odo gazed across the room, spotting Silas and Emmy sitting at a table playing cards. "No way, they're gambling?"

Chapter 40

Two Rivers

"Is that the Captain sitting with them?"

Odo and Sephie pushed through the bustling crowd to the card table where Silas and Emmy were sitting. Emmy looked up at them, waving. "Hi, guys. This is Captain Haynes, he owns the *Elysium Belle*. He was telling us about some of the famous people he's had as passengers. Like Mark Twain, for instance."

"Really? Mark Twain?"

Captain Haynes stood up, shaking Odo's hand, then Sephie's. "Captain David W. Haynes, at your service. A pleasure to meet you both, and welcome aboard the *Elysium Belle*, the finest sternwheeler to ever ply the Summerland River. Silas has been telling me about some of your marvelous adventures on other worlds. I must say it took me some time to get used to the astonishing variety of life forms in our universe, but I suppose in the end we're all the same."

Odo nodded. "I agree. We're headed to the River

Styx to see Charon the Ferryman. Your piano player said Charon might be closing his ferry business?"

"Quite true, and that is why I'm here with your two companions, to ask a favor of you. B9 told me you were on your way to see Charon. I wonder if you would be so kind as to deliver a letter to him? It's a proposition which I hope he will see in a favorable light."

"Sure, we can do that."

"Excellent." The Captain pulled a thick envelope from an inside coat pocket, handing it to Silas. "Have him contact me if this holds any interest for him. We stop for a few hours at Two Rivers on our way to the Land of the Dead. Charon's Crossing is about fifteen miles down the River Styx from there. Our final stop after Two Rivers is the Land of the Dead."

Odo said, "You've been there?"

"Indeed, many times."

"What's it like, exactly?"

"As you might guess, you are not the first person to ask me that question, and I shall give you the same answer I have given countless times before. There are no words in our language capable of describing the Land of the Dead. Some have said it's like trying to describe colors to a blind man, others, music to a deaf man. It can only be understood by experiencing it."

"Did you like it?"

"Did I like it? Not to befuddle you further, but it lies far beyond like or dislike, beyond all things, impossible to describe, as I said."

"At least now I know it's nothing at all like our

world. We'll be sure to give Charon your letter."

"Might I ask what your business is with him? You're not representing another passenger line, are you?"

"No, nothing like that. We're just returning something that belongs to him."

The Captain leaned back in his chair, scrutinizing Odo. "I see. If I may speak frankly, there is only one thing I can think of that Charon would like returned to him. A little advice, tell no one the purpose of your visit. There are, aboard this vessel, some unscrupulous scoundrels who would kill for such a prize as that."

"Someone already tried to take what we're returning to him. We won't let that happen again."

"It sounds as though it's in capable hands. I imagine the four of you make quite a formidable team. I wish you the best of luck. Please be my honored guests in the Presidential Suite for the rest of your journey. I think you'll find it quite comfortable, an escape from the constant noise and bedlam of the saloon." He handed a brass key to Odo.

"Thank you so much."

The Captain stood up, shaking their hands again. "A pleasure to meet you all. I shall be awaiting Charon's reply. I do believe it is a most beneficial proposition, hopefully one he will agree to."

Odo said, "I'm just curious. Were you a steamboat captain on Earth?"

"I was not, I captained an asteroid mining ship for many years, but it was always a dream of mine to pilot an old fashioned sternwheeler. Such is the nature of

Percupio."

"Wait, you're from the future, when people are mining asteroids? How can you be from the future?"

"How can you be from the past?"

"Percupio is definitely a strange place."

"You'll find none stranger, other than the Land of the Dead, of course."

For the next four days, they enjoyed the luxurious accommodations of the Presidential Suite, spending a great deal of time sitting on the hurricane deck watching the sights along the river, spotting lesson towns from a multitude of different eras. Odo's favorite was an ancient Roman town with a magnificent stone temple in its center. It was a town that Emmy was familiar with, but of course she couldn't tell them about her astonishing nocturnal flight over Percupio.

On the fifth day, the steam whistle blew four times, announcing their arrival at the sleepy little village of Two Rivers.

The Captain came down from the pilot house to see them off, giving them directions to Charon's Crossing, thanking them again for delivering his letter.

"Best of luck to you all. I imagine I shall be hearing a great deal about your future exploits."

They waved their good byes, heading down the ramp to Two Rivers, a handful of passengers debarking, only a few of those traveling on to Charon's Crossing.

"Wasn't the Presidential Suite amazing? My bed was so comfy. I've never had room service before."

Odo studied the almost deserted town. "Not many

people here. Most of the shops are boarded up."

Emmy said, "That gift shop is open."

"Great, more creepy centipedes?"

Sephie strode over to the store, peering in the window. "It's a regular gift shop, there's a clerk and a cash register."

Emmy opened the door and stepped inside, looking around the store. "What kind of souvenirs do you have? Do have any hats or tee shirts?"

"Are you headed to Charon's Crossing?"

"We are."

"You're all dead, then?"

Odo called out, "We're not dead, not even close to being dead."

"Of course, my mistake. The bad news is we don't have many souvenirs left, the good news is the ones we have are free. That shelf is full of promotional merchandise from Charon's Ferry, all free."

Emmy eyed the shelf. "These little wooden boats are free?"

"They are. They're replicas of Charon's ferry boat. I believe they were all shaped by a Fortisian, not hand carved, if that makes any difference to you."

"They're super nice." Emmy grabbed two of them, stuffing them into her pack.

Sephie said, "How come so many stores are boarded up?"

"Sadly, Two Rivers is not the tourist destination it once was. Every year fewer and fewer people are taking Charon's Ferry to the Land of the Dead. Most of the shops depended on the newly dead for business."

"How come they stopped coming here?"

"Charon's Crossing is not what it used to be; it's old and run down, his ferry hasn't been working right since Odysseus stole the Key Spike."

"How could a Key Spike make so much difference?"

"It's not just a spike, it warps space inside the cabin, making it much bigger on the inside than it is on the outside. He used to be able to carry hundreds of passengers on each trip. At one obolus per passenger, he was making a tidy sum of money on every crossing."

Sephie gave the clerk a bright smile. "We thought we'd go see Charon's Crossing just for fun. He really is kind of famous."

"You said you're not dead, correct?"

"Right, all four of us are alive."

"Charon's Crossing is about fifteen miles downriver, but I'm afraid you will have to pass through The Darkness to get there. It wouldn't be a problem if you were dead, of course, but since you're not, you should be… careful."

Chapter 41

The Darkness

Odo's eyes narrowed. "What is The Darkness? Why do we have to be careful?"

"You might get lost, bump into something."

Sephie said, "Thanks, we should be fine. I can shape some light orbs."

"I thought you might be a Fortisian, with that orange hair."

Odo wasn't giving up. "What exactly is The Darkness?"

"It's a one mile stretch of trail that is completely dark."

"Why is it dark?"

"No one knows for certain where it came from, but The Darkness has been there for at least three centuries. It's best if you walk briskly, not stopping for anything." The clerk raised one eyebrow.

"Are there creatures in it?"

"Some people may have seen wings flapping, heard singing. Remember, stop for nothing. Keep walking until you have passed through it. I can't emphasize this enough, no stopping for any reason."

Sephie studied the clerk's brainwaves. She was definitely not telling them everything, and she was frightened. "Thanks so much for your help. We won't stop."

Odo headed for the front door, picking up one of the little boat replicas. "This will look cool on my bookshelf at home."

As they strolled along the path leading to Charon's Crossing, Odo's eyes were on the other side of the river, almost a mile away. "That's the Land of the Dead over there?"

Silas nodded, "That's it, the other side of the River Styx."

"I can't see anything, it's just sort of blurry and foggy."

"Captain Haynes said it was impossible to describe."

"It looks like maybe there's a wall of clouds in front of it."

Odo turned to Silas. "Since you can see ghosts, maybe if you really focus on it you'll be able to see stuff in the Land of the Dead that we can't see."

"Maybe." Silas stopped, facing the river, his eyes focusing on the blurry wall of clouds.

"Do you see anything?"

He didn't answer, a strange frozen look on his face.

"What is it? What do you see?"

His voice was a whisper. "Where am I? What's happening?"

"Silas! What's wrong?"

Emmy grabbed his arm, shaking it. His eyes were glazed, his breathing shallow. "Silas! Wake up! Stop looking at it!"

Odo jumped in front of him, blocking his view.

A moment later Silas shook his head. "Nothing, just the big wall of clouds."

"It sounded like you saw something."

"Just clouds."

Sephie gave Odo a look. "We should get going." She knew Silas had seen something, something that made him forget where he was. She took Odo's hand, strolling along next to him.

Emmy walked next to Silas. "How do you feel?"

"I'm a little worried about The Darkness. It sounds kind of weird. She said something about wings flapping, which is a little creepy."

Emmy smiled. "We'll be fine, Sephie will make light orbs so we can see. Besides, she has all those amazing powers."

The path veered away from the river, taking them into a dense forest, the towering trees growing darker with each step they took.

"Is this it?"

Sephie nodded. "It's pitch black about fifty feet in front of us."

They headed into The Darkness, Sephie drawing three symbols in the air, a bright orb appearing in front of her, illuminating the trail.

Odo smiled. "Nice, not so scary now."

Silas stopped. "Do you hear that?"

Emmy tilted her head. "It's beautiful, someone is singing. I've never heard anything like it. What a lovely voice."

Odo nodded. "It is beautiful, enchanting. Let's stop and listen."

"No stopping, Odo Whitley. You heard the clerk at the gift shop."

A second voice joined in, harmonizing with the first.

Odo felt weak. "I have to sit down. That song… it's… it's so beautiful."

Silas slapped his forehead. "Sirens! It's the Sirens!"

Odo looked at him, his eyes barely focused. "It's not sirens, someone is singing. Why would there be sirens here?"

"Not that kind of sirens, Odo, it's the three Sirens who tried to lure Odysseus to his doom, tried to make him crash his ship onto the rocks. He only survived because Circe told his men to put wax in their ears. Sirens are half bird and half human, with wings. The lady at the gift shop said some people saw wings flapping."

Odo's eyes were closed. "Mmm… so beautiful."

Silas sank slowly to the ground. "The song… I can't fight it…"

Emmy was sitting on the forest floor, her head nodding. "So lovely… lovely…"

Sephie had her hands over her ears, studying their

brain waves. She'd have to be quick. She sang as loudly as she could to block the Sirens' song, then drew three symbols in the air, manipulating their neural pathways, paralyzing their auditory nerves, the four of them suddenly stone deaf.

Odo's eyes opened. Sephie could see his mouth moving but couldn't hear him. He looked angry. Silas stood up, saying something to Odo. Odo pointed to his ears, then to Sephie.

Emmy jumped up, grabbing Silas' arm, yelling something that no one could hear.

Sephie grabbed Odo's hand, dragging him down the trail, motioning for Emmy and Silas to follow them.

Ten minutes later they were standing in bright sunlight, Odo rubbing his ears. "I can hear again. How weird was that? That song was so amazing. Wait, do you think we could go back and record it on my phone? Think how much money we could make if we sold that song to a big music–"

Sephie reached out and flicked Odo's nose painfully with her finger. "Worst idea ever."

"Ow!"

Silas laughed. "Let's go, only another few miles to Charon's Crossing."

Odo rubbed his nose, looking at Sephie, raising one eyebrow. "It's showtime!"

Sephie nodded. "It is indeed."

Chapter 42

Charon's Crossing

Odo eyed the hand painted sign above the ramshackle wooden building.

Charon's Ferry
Reasonable rates • On time service
Fast and Safe Crossing!

Silas said, "Look at all the people waiting. Where's the ferry?"

Odo stepped over to an old man in a baggy black suit leaning against a tree, his head nodding.

"Hi, there."

The man blinked, rubbed his eyes, then said, "Good day to you, young sir."

"How often does the ferry cross over to the Land of the Dead?"

The old man seemed confused. "I don't really know. I think I've been waiting here for a long time, but it's hard to tell. You are from Earth? You're dead?"

"Not dead, but we are from Earth. We're trying to find Charon. You don't know how long you've been waiting? Have you seen Charon?"

"Let me think about this. Is Lincoln still president?"

"What?"

"Is Honest Abe still president?"

Odo shook his head. "No."

"Then it's been at least two years, maybe more."

"Right. Thanks for your help."

Odo ran back to the others. "That old guy has been waiting for the ferry since Lincoln was president."

"That's not good. He hasn't seen Charon?"

"No."

"We have to find him."

Emmy said, "His ferry isn't here, so maybe he's across the river in the Land of the Dead?"

"That would make sense. How do we get him to come back here? We can't wait around for two hundred years."

Silas said, "Sephie, can you shape me some binoculars? Maybe I can see his boat."

Odo said, "I have a small pair in my backpack. I'll look." He didn't want Silas going into that weird trance again.

He grabbed the binoculars, looking across the river. "I see something that could be a boat. It's hard to make it out in the fog."

Emmy said, "What should we do? How do we contact him?"

Odo eyed the river. "I can swim over. It's not that far and the river is really slow and calm. It's not at all like it was in my vision. Not even close."

"You're not swimming over there, it's too far."

"You can shape me a paddle board. I can lie on it and paddle across. I don't have to go into the Land of the Dead, I can get close and holler at him to get his attention."

"I don't know, Odo Whitley, it sounds kind of dangerous. I don't want anything to happen to you. You had that vision."

"I'll be fine, I'm an excellent swimmer and I'll have the paddle board."

"You have to promise me if it gets even a little bit cloudy or windy, you'll come right back?"

"I promise. There's not a cloud in the sky. In my vision there was a huge storm with thunder and lightning."

"Okay, but you have to be really careful."

"I promise."

Sephie drew two symbols, a four-foot long bright orange paddle board appearing in her hands. Odo took his shoes off and grabbed the board. He dipped his toes in the water. "It's nice and warm, not cold like it was in my vision." He pulled off his shirt and stepped into the river, lying down on the paddle board, pushing off. "The water's great. I'll be back in a flash. I'll catch a ride on Charon's boat."

"Be careful, Odo Whitley."

"I will."

Odo headed across the river. It was much easier than he thought it would be, nothing like his vision. The water was warm and calm with almost no current, like swimming in a bathtub. When he was almost halfway across he turned, calling out to Sephie, his voice carrying across the water.

"I'm fine, not tired at all!"

When he was precisely halfway between the Land of the Living and the Land of the Dead there was a sudden horrendously loud clap of thunder. Odo looked up, a horrible chill shooting through him. The sky was filled with black churning clouds. The deluge of rain came out of nowhere, then the howling wind, the rain blowing sideways, stinging his face, the water suddenly cold, wind blown waves crashing against him, pummeling him, almost knocking him off the board. He tried to turn around and head back to the Land of the Living, but he'd become disoriented, the howling wind and waves tossing him about. He wrapped his arms around the paddle board, holding on as tightly as he could. He could hear Sephie calling his name, her voice almost drowned out by the ferocious roaring wind.

He turned toward her voice, kicking as hard as he could, unable to tell if he was making any progress. Another wave crashed against him, slamming him back, ripping the paddle board from his grasp, the wind grabbing it, the orange board hurled wildly across the water, lost in the mountainous waves. Panic set in. His vision was coming true. He was going to drown, only this time he wouldn't wake up in his bed, he would

253

wake up in the Land of the Dead. His only hope was Charon's boat. This time he wouldn't let Charon hit him with the oar, this time he would tell him they had the–"

He let out a yelp when the boat crashed into him, knocking his head against the hard wooden hull. "Aggh!" He grabbed at the boat, just as he'd done in his vision.

When he looked up he saw Charon looking down at him with cold dark eyes.

"What are you doing here?"

"I'm drowning! Help me!"

"You don't belong here! There's no free lunches, boy!"

"You don't understand, we have your–"

Charon hit his hands with the heavy wooden paddle, Odo falling back into the churning water, a huge wave washing over him. He choked, gasping for air, another wave pushing Charon's boat away from him, Charon paddling off into the dark sheets of pounding rain. For the first time since they had arrived in Percupio, Odo was getting tired, the waves battering against him, his legs weak, his muscles burning. He wouldn't get to say good bye to Sephie. He rolled over, trying to float on his back, a massive cresting wave crashing onto him, pushing him under. He bobbed up to the surface again. He didn't have much time left. He was glad Sephie had the amulet. At least she would know how he felt about her. He should have told her sooner. He closed his eyes. That was the moment he heard the voice.

Chapter 43

Emmy's Surprise

Silas watched Odo paddling across the river. "He's a strong swimmer, he'll be fine."

"I know, but he had that vision."

"Maybe it was just sort of a weird distorted dream vision about Percupio."

"Maybe."

Emmy said, "He'll be back here in no time with Charon and the boat."

They sat on the shore, watching Odo paddle across the mile wide river.

"He's almost half way across and he's doing great."

Sephie smiled. "There's not a cloud in the sky."

All three of them jumped when the blinding bolt of lightning flashed, its thunderous report shaking the ground.

Sephie jumped to her feet. "The sky! It's all black! It's not possible! It was clear! Odo, come back! Odo!"

The pounding sheets of rain came, then the howling wind, five-foot waves crashing against the shore. Sephie fell to her knees when she lost sight of Odo. "No! Odo, come back! Please!"

Silas cried out, "I see the boat! I see Charon's boat! I think I see Odo!"

The three friends watched Charon raise his paddle, bringing it down, Odo disappearing into the waves, Charon paddling away from him.

Sephie's insides were ice cold, numb. Odo could drown. She would never see him again. Time seemed to slow to a horrible crawl.

"Sephie! Silas!"

Silas spun around. "What is it?"

Emmy had a strange look on her face, one he had never seen before. "I'm going to save him, Silas. I'm going to save Odo."

"What?"

She held out both arms, transforming her body. Her legs were straight, strong. She knew the Sinarian would take away her power to fly, but she didn't care, she was not going to let anything happen to her friends; not Odo, not Sephie, and not Silas. She floated up, Silas' jaw dropping.

"Emmy?"

She soared upward, then shot across the water, disappearing into the deluge of rain. She shielded her eyes, trying to spot Odo. She knew he was halfway across the river, knew she was close, but it was hard to see with the huge waves and whitecaps and rain. She saw a brown shape about twenty feet in front of her and flew toward it. It was Charon's boat. She dropped down low, traveling in the opposite direction of the boat, back to where it had been.

She gave a shout when she saw him, a wave pushing him under. He floated back up again, gasping for breath. Seconds later she was hovering above him.

"Odo, take my hand!"

He looked up at her, unable to comprehend what he was seeing.

Emmy reached down and grabbed his hand. When he would tell the story later on, he would always say that the moment Emmy grabbed his hand was the moment everything changed. His body was suddenly light, it felt effortless when he floated up into the air. It was incredible.

He wasn't going to die, he wasn't going to leave Sephie, he could go home, see his parents, go back to school, go to the movies–

"Odo, are you okay?"

"You can fly. You're flying. We're flying."

Emmy nodded, "I know. The Sinarian said I wasn't supposed to tell you guys, but I couldn't let anything happen to you. Silas and Sephie and you are my best friends in the world."

"How come I'm floating? I feel light, like I don't have a body."

"When we hold hands your body becomes part of me, connected to me. It's transformed the same way I transform my own body."

They flashed across the water, the storm instantly vanishing when they passed the halfway mark. Odo hollered out to Sephie, "I'm okay! Emmy can fly!"

When they landed on the sandy shore Sephie threw her arms around Odo. "I thought you were gone... I didn't think I'd see you again."

"I thought it was all over. All I could think about was you."

Silas was staring at Emmy. "You can fly. You can seriously fly, and not just in your dreams. Why didn't you tell us?"

"A Sinarian made me promise not to tell. He said he would take away my power to fly if I did."

"Your legs are straight. How is that possible?"

"I have control over my body. I can turn it into a dream body, make it be whatever I want."

Odo looked at Emmy. "You're going to lose your power because you rescued me?"

"I had it when I needed it most. That's all I care about."

Sephie stepped over to Emmy, giving her a long hug. "You saved Odo, you saved me."

"You would have done the same for me."

Sephie nodded. "In a heartbeat."

Odo couldn't stop looking at Emmy. "I can't believe you can fly. That's so completely amazing. Can you fly on Earth?"

"I don't think I'll get the chance to find out. The Sinarian was really serious about taking the power away if I showed you guys. He said I'd never fly again, ever."

The four friends turned when they heard shouting, a crowd of people running toward Charon's boat. Charon lashed it to the dock, climbing out of the boat.

A sudden and terrible burning rage tore through Odo when he saw Charon. Charon had tried to kill him, tried to push him under the water, tried to drown him, take him away from Sephie, from his parents. He would pay for that. He wished he had Sephie's powers. He would obliterate Charon, vaporize him where he stood, crush him like a —"

"Odo! Stop! You have to stop!"

Odo spun around. "You're reading my brain waves?"

"I am, and I don't like what I'm seeing. You need to be Odo Whitley, not Charon. Be the person who gave me the gold locket."

Odo couldn't take his eyes off Charon. "He tried to kill me."

"So now you want to kill him, be just like him, be a murderer? Be Odo the Translucent Murderer?"

"I was scared, I thought I was going to die. I thought I'd never see you again."

"Maybe it was no accident that the Sinarian taught Emmy how to fly. Maybe he knew. Maybe Wikerus knew. Maybe they all knew."

"I meant what I said in the locket. I should have told you sooner."

"I know."

Silas' eyes were on Charon. "What are we going to do about him? He tried to kill Odo."

Sephie said, "We're going to give him the Key Spike and bring Jacob back to the Land of the Living. That's the only thing that matters. It's why we're here."

"You're right. Let's get this over with."

The four friends headed down to the dock, pushing through the crowd to Charon. Odo stepped up to him, his expression cold, emotionless. "We have your Key Spike. We want to bring someone back from the Land of the Dead."

Charon took a step back. "You're the one who tried to swim across to the Land of the Dead without filling out the paperwork."

Chapter 44

Charon the Ferryman

Odo stared at Charon. "What?"

"Do you know how much trouble I would be in if you crossed over without filling out all the forms? I'd lose my ferry license."

"What are you talking about? You tried to kill me."

Charon rolled his eyes. "You can't kill someone who's already dead, nimbus."

"I'm not dead."

The color drained from Charon's face. "Oh, dear. You're not dead?"

Sephie said, "You thought he was dead? You pushed him under the water because you thought nothing would happen to him?"

"He tried to cross over without paying my fee, without filling out all the paperwork. I didn't know you were alive. I'm sorry, truly sorry. I had no idea."

Odo stared at Charon. He wanted so badly to be

angry at him, wanted someone, anyone, to pay for scaring him like that. "You really thought I was dead?"

"You must understand, there hasn't been a living person at Charon's Crossing in at least two hundred years, just people waiting to cross over to the Land of the Dead. I'm so sorry. I'll do anything I can to make it up to you."

Odo pulled the Key Spike from his pack, handing it to Charon. "We want to bring someone back from the Land of the Dead."

"Give me a name and it will be done. I'll take care of all the paperwork, make sure everything goes smoothly. You are from Earth?"

Emmy stepped forward,. "Yes, we're from Earth. I want to bring back my brother, Jacob Snow."

Charon rubbed his chin, his gaze distant. "It was a car accident? A young boy about your age when he crossed over? His father had been drinking?"

Emmy gave a start. "You remember him? You know about the accident, about my dad?"

"I remember everyone. It is a curse and a blessing, as are most gifts. There is so much sadness, but also great joy when they reach the Land of the Dead and finally understand."

"Oh."

"Your brother Jacob is fine, doing well. I believe he has spent a great deal of time on Earth since he passed."

"Silas saw him there. He can see ghosts. Jacob showed us the Key Spike, he wanted us to find it."

"I see."

Emmy's voice was almost a whisper. "Will I die in the accident instead of him? Will I take his place in the Land of the Dead, exchange my life for his?"

"Good heavens, what would the point of that be? It's nothing like that at all. Everything will be fine, seamless, I'll make certain of it. You have my word, nothing to worry about, I promise."

Charon took the Key Spike, stepping over to his boat, inserting it into the bow. The spike glowed with a pale green light. "It's done." He called out to the crowd of people milling about on the dock. "All aboard! This is your lucky day, your crossing is free, no charge." He nodded to Odo.

They watched as over ninety people entered the small cabin on Charon's boat.

Silas said, "That's so weird that it's bigger inside than it is on the outside."

Sephie said, "Charon, how long will you be? We have to talk to you about something else."

"I'll be back within the hour."

Odo watched as an unseen force propelled the boat across the water, Charon standing on the bow. "I wonder what it's like over there? I know Captain Haynes said it was impossible to describe, but I wish I knew. It's going to drive me crazy."

Sephie took his hand. "That's why Bob the Mechanic gives you such hard questions, questions you can't possibly answer."

"What do you mean?"

"He's trying to teach you that some questions are

impossible to answer, that you have to accept that, let them go and move on with your life."

Odo nodded. "I know not every question can be answered, but why do you think he–"

"Let it go, Odo Whitley."

"Sorry."

Emmy said, "How about we all get a bird's eye view of Percupio before the Sinarian takes away my power?"

Silas gave a yelp. "Yes! That would be amazing!" He grabbed Emmy's hand.

Odo and Sephie darted over, all four of them holding hands.

"Is everyone ready? All holding hands?"

"Of course we are, let's go!"

Emmy closed her eyes for a moment, her body transforming into a dream body, her legs straight again. Sephie gave a shriek when she was suddenly weightless, floating up into the air. "Is this safe?"

"As long as we're holding hands we're good. If you did let go, I could fly down and grab you."

The four friends soared up into the green sky, the land spreading out before them as far as they could see. "Look at the Summerland River, look how far it goes!"

"Odo pointed to the River Styx. "It goes in a circle around the Land of the Dead, like a moat around a castle. Shouldn't the Land of the Dead be a lot bigger? It's all cloudy."

"That circular area is probably a doorway to the Land of the Dead."

"But how could it possibly–"

"Some questions have no answers, Odo Whitley."

Emmy laughed. "So many unsolved mysteries. I never realized how big the universe was, how many worlds and dimensions there are."

"Can you fly us up the Summerland River? Maybe we'll see the *Elysium Belle*."

They shot forward, flashing across the land, following the Summerland River.

"The giant black wall is gone! So is Paradise Falls!"

Silas was the first to spot the steamboat, it's huge paddle wheel churning up the water. "There's the *Elysium Belle*! Fly down over it. Let's wave to Captain Haynes."

They streaked through the sky, then floated down fifty feet above the paddle wheeler. Odo hollered, "Captain Haynes!"

They watched as he stepped out of the pilot house, first looking around him, then up, his jaw dropping when he saw the four friends floating above the ship. He waved to them, darting back into the pilot house, the steam whistle blasting out seconds later. He stepped out again, waving.

Emmy said, "We should head back. Charon is probably waiting for us."

"Fly down for a second so I can talk to the Captain."

They floated down, now only ten feet above the ship.

Odo called out, "We found Charon, we're going to give him your letter as soon as we get back. He had to ferry a group to the Land of the Dead. We gave him the Key Spike."

"Wonderful! You can fly! You never mentioned that!"

"We just found out ourselves. We have to go, thanks again for everything."

"Have a grand time! I hope to see you all again!"

The four friends soared up, shooting across the sky toward Charon's Crossing.

Ten minutes later Odo called out, "I can see Charon's boat! He's coming back!"

Chapter 45

The Letter

Charon waved to them as they floated down to the dock.

"This is most astonishing. You can fly?"

"Emmy can. She's the one who rescued me from the water."

"I'm glad she was there for you. It was a mistake I will never make again, I promise you."

"We have a letter for you from Captain David W. Haynes, owner and captain of the *Elysium Belle.*"

Charon's expression darkened. "No doubt gloating about the stunning success of his steamboat business. Your Captain Haynes has taken away most of my passengers. I used to ferry many hundreds of people a day across the River Styx, but those days are over. I'll wager he wants to buy my ferry so he can shut it down for good."

Sephie said, "I don't think so. He's actually a very

nice person. He said the letter is a business proposition for you, one he thinks you'll like."

Charon sniffed. "We'll see."

Sephie pulled the envelope from her pack, handing it to Charon. He opened it, studying the thick sheath of papers.

"It's a contract of some kind." He sat down on the dock, dangling his feet in the River Styx, reading the long document. Finally he folded it up, sliding it into a pocket in his cloak.

"What did he say?"

"He wants me to go into business with him, be a partner in his steamship line. He called me a legend, said everyone knows my name. He is building a second steamship and will name it the Charon, said I would be the captain. He'll teach me how to run it."

"That's amazing. What do you think?"

Charon stood up, his wooden boat rocking gently in the water. "I think it's time to catch up to a changing world. It's time to move on."

Emmy said, "All transitions are chaotic and scary."

Charon nodded. "Quite true, young lady. I am both frightened and excited. Never in my wildest dreams did I imagine I would be the captain of a steamboat."

"A steamboat named after you. You'll get to wear a cool uniform, dark blue with shiny brass buttons. And a cool hat."

"I suppose it's about time to shed this old cloak of mine. It's almost two thousand years old."

"Whoa." Odo glanced over at Sephie, grimacing.

Charon said, "Might I ask one last favor?"

"Of course."

"Would you fly to the *Elysium Belle* and tell Captain Haynes that I have decided to accept his generous offer and will meet him tomorrow at Two Rivers to discuss the details and sign the contract?"

Odo grinned. "Any excuse to fly is fine with me."

The four friends bid farewell to Charon, soaring up into the skies above Percupio.

"Let's go take a look at that cool Roman temple."

Silas said, "It looked like the Roman Pantheon, the temple they built to all their gods."

"I can't believe they thought Zeus used to throw lightning bolts when he got angry."

Silas considered mentioning Madam Futura the palm reader, then decided against it. Too soon.

"Whoa, look over there, it's an Egyptian pyramid!"

"That's amazing!"

"There's a sphinx behind it!"

It took the friends over seven hours to reach the *Elysium Belle*, stopping at dozens of remarkable structures along the way. Odo purchased a small stone carving of Zeus from a vendor next to the Pantheon, holding it up for the others to see. "I'll use this as a waystone in case we want to come back here sometime. We can visit Charon, see how he looks in a captain's uniform, maybe take a ride on his steamboat."

When they finally landed on the *Elysium Belle*, they gave Captain Haynes the news that Charon had accepted his proposal of partnership.

"Marvelous, simply marvelous! His name alone will bring in two or three times as many passengers as we have now. I may have to build a third steamboat. I wonder if Mark Twain would be interested? Hmm, one step at a time, I suppose."

The four friends stood on the upper deck of the *Elysium Belle*, gazing across the sparkling Summerland River.

"This was the most incredible, and sometimes scariest, adventure yet."

Silas turned to Emmy. "What do you think? Do you still want to be part of our group, *The Incredible Ghostwatcher and his Three Anonymous Friends*?"

She glanced at Sephie and Odo. "We might need to tweak that name a little, but yes, I would love to be part of your group."

"We make an incredible team."

Sephie nodded, taking Odo's hand. "We do indeed."

Odo gave Silas an innocent smile. "You never did tell us what the inscription was on the watch Emmy gave you. I bet it was something nice."

"I didn't tell you? Sorry, my bad." Silas took his watch off, flipping it over. "Um, it says, *None of Odo Whitley's business.*"

Odo snorted.

Sephie said, "I guess it's time to head home."

Emmy grabbed her pack, slinging it onto her shoulder. "I'm really excited, but also scared about Jacob coming back. I don't know how it's going to work. How are we going to explain it to everyone?"

TOM HOFFMAN

"Charon said it would be seamless. It will be fine. He's been doing this for thousands of years."

"Is everyone ready?"

They all held hands, Odo pulling his homestone from under his shirt. "Fasten your seatbelts, it's showtime."

"That makes no sense, Odo Whitley. What do seatbelts have to do with showtime, and why would–"

There was a brilliant flash of light and the four friends vanished, leaving the astonishing world of Percupio behind them.

Emmy felt slightly dizzy when they blinked into Wikerus Praevian's sitting room. "I don't think I'll ever get used to that."

"It takes a while, but you will. Wait, can you fly?"

Emmy raised her arms, her body transforming. She floated up off the ground, then back down. "I can fly, but I have a feeling I'll be seeing the Sinarian very soon."

"You're back! How did it go?" They turned to see Wikerus and Mrs. Preke step into the room.

"It was scary and amazing, but we made it back safely. We returned the Key Spike to Charon and he's going to bring Jacob back to the Land of the Living. He said it would be seamless, that there was nothing for Emmy to worry about."

"Excellent. You can tell us all about your trip after you get a good night's sleep and everything returns to normal."

Mrs. Preke said, "It's lovely to see you all, and I'm

so glad your adventure was successful. It's especially nice to meet you, Emmy. Wikerus has told me so much about you, and what a remarkable person you are. If you're interested, there's a job waiting for you at Serendipity Salvage."

Odo whispered loudly, "You'll make a ton of money."

Emmy grinned. "It sounds like so much fun, I'd love to work there."

Silas stepped over to Mrs. Preke, whispering something in her ear. She glanced at Emmy. "Are you sure? I don't want to frighten her."

Emmy said, "Silas, what are you doing?"

"There's something I thought you should see. You remember how I told you Mrs. Preke was a Plindorian formshifter?"

"Yes."

"Check this out." He nodded to Mrs. Preke.

She shimmered, her body flowing and translucent. A moment later she transformed into a six-foot tall yellow octopus.

Emmy gave a shriek, clapping her hand over her mouth, the others laughing.

"That's what Plindorians look like. They don't live in the ocean though, and they have a lot of cool technology."

Mrs. Preke said, "It's still just me, no matter what form I take."

Emmy said, "That might be the coolest thing I've ever seen."

"We should go. Only an hour has passed since we left, but I told my mom I wouldn't be long."

"I'll see you all at school tomorrow and let you know how everything goes at home. I don't know if Jacob will be there, how long it will be until he comes back."

Sephie gave her a hug. "It will be fine, I know it will."

Emmy attempted a smile, but she had no idea what she would say to Jacob when she saw him, or what she would say to her mom.

Chapter 46

Jacob

Emmy stopped outside her front gate, no idea what would be waiting for her inside. If Jacob was there, would he be the same age he was when he died? Would her mom be freaking out, thinking she was going crazy? She sighed. She could almost hear Silas telling her there was only one way to find out. She stepped onto the front porch, taking a deep breath, reaching for the doorknob.

An astonishing thing happened when she touched it. She doubled over, her head spinning, her thoughts wildly confused, a lifetime of memories flooding through her in less than a second. She stood up, shaking, trying to understand what was happening to her. She stumbled over to the porch swing and sat down. This couldn't be, and yet it was. She looked down at her legs. They were straight, and she hadn't transformed to her dream body. They had always been straight. The accident had never happened, at least not the way she remembered it.

They had swerved off the road, but there was no ravine, they just skidded to a stop, her mom yelling at her dad, saying he could have killed them all. Jacob was fine, she was fine. They drove home and two months later her dad left. She hadn't seen him since.

She stood up, opening the front door, this time knowing what to expect.

Jacob and two friends were sitting on the couch in front the big TV playing a video game, a half eaten pizza on the coffee table. He didn't even look up, just called out, "Hey, Em! Did you ace the math test?"

She wanted to run over and hug him and never let go, but she couldn't. He had no memory of dying, of being a ghost, of being in the Land of the Dead. He'd think she was a total lunatic if she told him what had happened.

"Of course I aced it. Did you hear from Gonzaga?"

"Yeah, nothing surprising, I got accepted, got a full scholarship."

Emmy let out a shriek. "No way! Mom's going to go crazy!"

"I already called her, she wants us to go to dinner and celebrate."

"That sounds great, it'll be fun."

"She sold that crazy haunted house. It has a secret room in the basement."

"How fun would that be, living in a haunted house with a secret room?"

"Uh, totally creepy and not fun at all?"

Emmy laughed. "I have to go study."

"Have fun, nerd."

Emmy ran upstairs to her room, looking around. There were some pictures on the wall of her and Jacob when they were growing up. She froze when she saw a picture of her standing next to a boy, his arm around her. She had a boyfriend, and his name wasn't Silas.

She sank down on her bed, her stomach in knots. She liked Alex, he was funny and a great basketball player, but he was nothing like Silas. Silas was the most amazing person she'd ever met. He could see ghosts and he'd traveled to other dimensions and other worlds, his grandpa was an incredible inventor. When he had showed her the inscription on the watch she gave him, she said it was all true.

She lay back on her bed. This was so confusing. Everything was different. She was popular at school, no one made fun of her or felt sorry for her. They all wanted to be friends with her. She remembered seeing Sephie in the hall, thinking she should dye her hair, anything except that crazy orange color. She remembered Silas as a shy brainiac in her science class who she'd never talked to. He always looked like he was worried about something. She knew now that he was seeing ghosts, probably grandparents of some of the kids, probably talking to them, helping them move on. She'd never even noticed Odo, but she did have a vague memory of Sephie walking down the hall with some-one, probably Odo.

She looked at the phone on her desk, a new smart phone her mom had gotten her for her birthday. She could call Silas, but what would she say? Hey, Silas, I have a boyfriend named Alex, and he's a super good basketball player, really popular. She groaned, pulling the pillow over her face. Maybe she should call Sephie and ask her what to do.

A thought popped into her head. She knew it was from her deeper self, from Nomi. She should follow her heart, follow the path that brings her joy. Be true to herself.

The world she was returning to was the world she had always dreamed about, but she knew now it wasn't the world for her. Knowing Silas and Sephie and Odo had changed everything. Tomorrow was going to be a very busy day, and like all big transitions, it was going to be chaotic and scary.

Silas ran all the way to the school bus. He couldn't wait to find out what happened with Jacob, to see how Emmy was doing. He hopped onto the bus and ran down the aisle, stopping when he saw the boy sitting next to her. Emmy was talking to him, and he had his hand on her arm.

Silas felt sick, slumping down into an empty seat, his insides twisted into knots. She was sitting next to Alex Underwood, the star basketball player, one of the most popular kids in school. What was happening? He whipped around when he heard someone call out, "Hey, Jacob! Way to go on getting into Gonzaga."

Emmy called out, "He got a full scholarship!"

"Nice! We should celebrate after school."

Silas wanted to shrink down until he disappeared. He wished he was a shifter like Odo. He could go back to Percupio. Except Emmy wouldn't be there.

When the bus squealed to a halt, Silas hopped off, standing behind a parked car, waiting for Emmy. She stepped down, still talking to Alex. Silas gave a start when he saw her legs. They were straight. Had she transformed her body? Two girls ran up to her, whispering in her ear, all three of them laughing.

"No way, really? He said that?"

They headed toward the front door, Silas walking behind them. He followed them into the school, followed them to Emmy's locker. He didn't know what to do. Would she even remember him? Had something happened, was it a new timeline where they had never met? She was so popular now, she'd never even look at him.

He ran down the hallway, turned around and began walking slowly back. Alex was gone, it was just Emmy and her two friends walking toward him. She wasn't looking at him, just laughing and talking. It was his turn to be the translucent boy. This must be how Odo felt every day.

He looked down, unable to make eye contact with her. When she bumped into him he dropped his backpack. She reached down and picked it up, handing it to him.

"Sorry!"

Then she was gone.

Chapter 47

The Note

When the lunch bell rang, Odo and Sephie headed to the cafeteria. As they walked toward their usual table in the back, Sephie stopped short, grabbing Odo's arm. "Look, two tables over."

"What's Emmy doing? Is she friends with those guys? Where's Silas?"

"Look at her legs."

"They're straight. Is that her dream body?"

"I don't think so. We need to find Silas."

They headed over to their table, spotting Silas sitting alone, eating his lunch. Odo sat down across from him. "Why is Emmy sitting with those kids?"

Silas shook his head. "She doesn't remember me. She walked right past me without saying anything, didn't even look at me. Jacob is back, I heard them saying he got a full scholarship to Gonzaga."

Sephie said, "It must be a new timeline, maybe one

where the accident never happened."

"And one where she never met me."

"Your watch! You're wearing the watch she gave you. How could that happen if she never met you?"

Silas shrugged. "I don't know, it doesn't matter. She doesn't know who I am and there's no way she'll ever talk to me. She was sitting next to Alex Underwood on the bus. He had his hand on her arm."

"Oh." Odo looked at Sephie.

Sephie said, "Maybe I could try talking to her."

"She probably doesn't remember you either."

"Maybe you could just say hello or something, you know, just be friendly. See what happens."

"Tell her I see ghosts? I don't think so. It's over and I'd better get used to it."

Odo said, "Why don't you come over after school? We can hang out."

"Thanks, but I need to think about some stuff."

"I get it. Call me if you want to talk."

"I will."

The day dragged on, Silas seeing Emmy in the hall twice with her friends. It looked like she was having a lot of fun. He was glad she had a lot of friends, but it also made him feel sick inside.

The last bell finally rang, Silas grabbing his pack and heading for the bus. He was standing in line when someone bumped into him from behind. He turned, freezing. It was Emmy. She gave him a strange look. "What are you doing?"

He blinked, no idea what she meant. "Uh, sorry, was

I in your way?"

A look of fear flitted across her face. She whispered, "In my way?"

"What?"

They stood motionless, neither wanting to be the first to talk. Emmy pointed to his wrist. "I like your watch."

"You like my watch?"

"What does the inscription say?"

Silas felt his body turning to jello, his legs wobbly. He whispered, "You remember?"

She reached over and grabbed his pack, pulling out a piece of paper from a side pocket, holding it up in front of him.

> *Meet me after school. We have to talk.*
> *Jacob is back. -Emmy*

"I put this in your pack when I bumped into you this morning."

"You remember everything? Percupio?"

"Of course I do, how could I forget?"

"I thought it was a different timeline, one where you never met me, where you didn't know who I was. It was awful."

She grabbed his hand. "I remember everything. I remember both timelines, the one with the accident where Jacob died, and the new one where no one was hurt. I didn't know you or Sephie or Odo in the new timeline, but I remembered you from the old one."

"Are you... um... on the bus... I saw you sitting with Alex Underwood?"

"I broke up with him this morning. I told him I'd met someone else."

"Really? You'd go out with me instead of him? He's super handsome and an athlete and people like him and–"

"He doesn't see ghosts and he doesn't make me laugh like you do and he doesn't understand things like you do and he's never seen an alien. You're amazing, Silas. Anytime you think you're not, just look at the back of your watch."

"So are you, amazing. You can fly, you're not afraid of giant yellow Plindorians or big green centipedes or gunfights in steamboat saloons."

Emmy laughed. "Eat lead, lizard face."

Silas smiled, studying her face. "I know what your superhero name is. I just thought of it."

"Lizard Face?"

Silas shook his head. "Dream Girl."

Emmy blinked. "That is so perfect, I love it. Ghost-watcher and Dream Girl. We're superheroes just like Odo and Sephie."

"Have you seen the Sinarian? Did he take away your power yet?"

"Not yet. I'm not sure when he'll show up. Odo and Sephie said Sinarians are really unpredictable."

"They got that right. Is it weird to have Jacob back?"

"It's not strange at all because I remember the time-line when he wasn't hurt. I remember growing up with him, I have pictures in my room. It's like I've had two different lives as different people, shy Emmeline with the crooked legs and popular Emmy with lots of friends. Shy Emmeline always wished she was popular Emmeline, but when I was popular Emmeline it felt kind of empty, like something was always missing. It felt like I was always homesick. Having you and Sephie and Odo for friends was the best thing that ever happened to me. I wouldn't give that up for anything."

"I was so scared when I thought you didn't remember me, didn't know me. I didn't know what to do."

The bus door opened, the kids crowding in, Silas and Emmy taking a seat. A girl stopped next to them, looking at Silas, then Emmy. She whispered to Emmy, "I heard you broke up with Alex. Is this your new boyfriend?"

Emmy nodded. "This is Silas. He's pretty cool, super smart."

"And cute." The girl grinned, winking at Silas, watching his face turn bright red. "See you tomorrow, Em."

"See you."

Emmy pulled her phone out. "I just got a text from Mrs. Preke. We're supposed to go see Wikerus tomorrow."

"Can I borrow your phone for a second? I want to text Odo." She handed Silas the phone, watching as he typed the message.

She remembers everything. Her name is Dream Girl.

Chapter 48

Emmy's Name

The next day was Saturday, Odo jumping out of bed when his alarm went off, rubbing his hands together. It was going to be a good day. They were going to see Wikerus in the morning, then go to a movie in the afternoon. Sephie had even let him choose the movie. He got dressed and grabbed his backpack, taking out his souvenirs from Percupio.

He wrapped the Zeus figurine in a soft cloth, putting it in the box of waystones he'd gotten from Madam Malitia. The little wooden model of Charon's boat went on his bookshelf.

"Nice. I can't believe we actually met Charon the Ferryman. I hope we read about him in history class." He imagined himself correcting the teacher, telling her that Charon was currently a steamboat captain on the Summerland River in Percupio. He laughed. That story would end with him in the principal's office.

He ran downstairs, darting into the kitchen, forgetting to make his grand bombastic announcement. His mom was sitting at the table reading a book. He said, "What are you reading?"

She gave a start, slamming the book shut, putting her arms over it. "You gave me a fright. What would you like for breakfast? Are you famished?"

Odo stared at her. "Am I famished?"

"It means really hungry."

"I know what it means. What were you reading?"

"Just some old book."

"What kind of old book?"

Petunia whispered, "You can't tell your dad."

"What is it? Is something wrong?"

"I'm taking an English class at Gardner College." She took her arms off the book.

"You're reading *Pride and Prejudice?*"

"It's for my class. The author is Jane Austen, she lived in England in the 1800s. The protagonist is named Elizabeth Bennet."

Odo said, "That's fantastic! How come you don't want to tell Dad? I think it's amazing. Are you going to get a degree?"

Petunia gave an embarrassed grin, "I hadn't really thought that far ahead. I just wanted to improve my vocabulary. I've never forgotten I didn't know what translucent meant when I read the note on the perfume bottle."

"Don't worry about that. I like being translucent, I have good friends who can see me, and it's fun. Most of the time I don't even think about it. I think it's amazing that you're taking the class. You should tell Dad, he'd be proud of you."

"Maybe after I finish this class. I want to see how it goes."

"You'll do great, your vocabulary is really improving."

"Thanks, King Odo. How about waffles for breakfast?"

When breakfast was done, Odo grabbed his pack, saying, "I'm going to go hang out with my friends. We're going to the movies this afternoon."

"Say hello to Sephie for me. And Silas."

"I will."

Odo headed out the door, walking toward Expergo Street. Mrs. Preke said they should all be there at exactly 10:30, but she didn't say why.

Silas, Emmy, and Sephie were standing on the sidewalk outside the old Victorian mansion when Odo arrived.

"Hey, Odo!"

He waved to them. "Does anyone know what this is about?"

"Not a clue."

Emmy said, "We're not in trouble are we?"

"I don't think so. Wikerus didn't mention anything when we got back."

They knocked on the door, Mrs. Preke pulling it open. "There you are, right on time. Wikerus is waiting for you in the sitting room."

"How come he wants to see us? Is anything wrong?"

"He'll explain everything. We're having a very special visitor today."

"Who?"

"Follow me."

They headed down the hallway into the sitting room, Wikerus in his favorite stuffed armchair reading an ancient leather bound book. "Ah, there you are. Excellent. Take a seat please." He pulled a gold watch from his vest pocket, studying it. "Any moment now." He smiled at them, drumming his fingers on the arm of the chair.

Mrs. Preke was standing beside him, also smiling.

Odo looked over at Sephie, raising his eyebrows.

She shook her head.

The air shimmered with an orange light just before the Sinarian appeared, floating silently six inches above the floor.

Emmy's heart sank. She knew why Wikerus had asked them to be there. The Sinarian was going to take her power away. Wikerus was probably angry that she had told the others she could fly.

"We are pleased with you."

Wikerus smiled. "It is a great honor indeed to have you here."

"I am here to speak with Emmeline."

Emmy felt sick. Silas held her hand. "It will be okay."

"We are not taking away your power."

Emmy stared at the Sinarian. "But I told the others I could fly."

287

"When you saw Odo drowning in the river, you knew the only way to save him would mean revealing your ability to the others. You also knew you would lose your power because of this, but you chose to do it anyway. In doing so, you held someone else's life far above your own personal gain, your own personal power. There is nothing more noble than that. We will not be taking away your ability to transform your body."

Emmy's eyes welled up. "Thank you so much."

"Besides risking your lives to bring Jacob back to the Land of the Living, you have brought about great change to Percupio, far deeper change than you are aware of. You are together again, all four of you, and many grand adventures lay before you. You will change your world and a thousand others through your bravery, friendship, and kindness. We are pleased with you. A gift of great joy and great sorrow; what was lost has now been found."

Odo said, "That was you? You were the voice I heard in my vision? What exactly was lost? And what was found? Are you talking about Jacob? About Emmy?"

There was a flash of orange light and the Sinarian was gone, the room silent.

Emmy said, "They're not taking away my power. I can't believe it, I was so worried."

Wikerus said, "It is a singular event when a Sinarian pays a visit, and rarer indeed when he says they are pleased with you. You have done well, Mrs. Preke and I are proud of you all."

Odo said, "Did you notice he said the four of us were all together *again*? Why did he say *again*? What did that mean?"

Wikerus smiled. "Perhaps he was confused, he is quite old, Odo."

Odo knew there was no way a Sinarian would be confused about anything. "Right, he's just a little old confused Sinarian."

Sephie scanned Wikerus' brain waves, but he was blurring them. She scanned Mrs. Preke's brain waves. She was extremely amused about something.

Wikerus got up from his armchair, putting his hand on Odo's shoulder. "Well done, all of you."

Silas whispered something to Emmy, then started chanting, "Do it, do it, do it!"

Emmy held her arms out, floating up off the floor, circling the room, then landing again, a huge grin on her face.

Everyone clapped, Silas calling out, "Three cheers for Dream Girl, the amazing new superhero!"

Emmy laughed, taking a bow. "Now that I'm officially a superhero, I think our group needs a name."

"We already have one, *The Amazing Translucent Boy and his Three Sidekicks*."

"Don't ever say that again, Odo Whitley." Sephie scanned Emmy's brainwaves. She was excited, happy, nervous, and there was something she wanted to say.

Silas said, *"What happened to Ghostwatcher and his Three Anonymous Friends?"*

Everyone stared at him.

"Fine, we don't have to use that one."

Sephie said, "I think Dream Girl has a name for us."

Emmy was shifting nervously from one foot to the other. "Well, I did think of one, but you might not like it."

"Dream Girl and her Three Little Pals?"

Sephie punched Odo's arm. "Knock it off."

Emmy said, "There's something that we all have in common."

"We're all super cool?"

"It's kind of the opposite of that. We've all experienced really difficult times in our lives, but we made it through them. We rose from the ashes to be who we are now."

Odo nodded, "That's true. I was translucent and alone, and Sephie lost her parents when she was little. Kids at school used to call her mean names. We were outsiders, never fit in with all the other kids."

Silas said, "I saw ghosts and was afraid of everything."

"I lost my brother, had crooked legs, and used to hide from the world in the Cube. Everything we went through made us the people we are now, but it also made us... a little bit odd."

Odo nodded. "Silas and Sephie are super odd."

Silas glared at Odo. "Said the translucent kid who can walk through walls. Talk about odd. You're odd squared, maybe even odd cubed."

Odo snorted, then said, "Emmy does have a point, we're all a little bit odd, especially Silas. He's actually

290

closer to super weird than odd."

"What's that supposed to mean?"

Odo said, "Just kidding. I remember something that Wikerus said to me when I was six years old, sitting in my front yard playing with the six-wheeled sailing truck he gave me for my birthday. My dad thought the truck was weird and he didn't want me to play with it, but it was my favorite toy. Wikerus said that sometimes weird things turn out to be the most precious things in our lives, the things we cherish above all others."

Sephie blinked. "Are you trying to make us cry, Odo Whitley?"

Odo shook his head. "I'm just saying odd isn't always a bad thing, and in our case, it's a very good thing."

"That's true, we're all odd, but we're also amazing, and the best friends ever."

Emmy said, "I think we should call ourselves *The Odd Squad.*"

Odo burst out laughing.

Sephie grinned.

Silas nodded. "I love it. It's totally us."

Odo said, "The Odd Squad it is. Now, as you all know, every group needs a leader, and since I was really the one who–"

"Zip it, Odo Whitley. No leaders in this group, just four amazing friends having amazing adventures."

Chapter 49

Mushroom People

Odo and Sephie were strolling down Expergo Street on their way home from the movie.

Sephie said, "None of that made sense. The mushroom people couldn't have come from the center of the Earth; the Earth's core is solid rock and six thousand degrees, the outer core is about five thousand degrees, and the Earth's mantle is two thousand degrees."

"Maybe they're cold blooded creatures like lizards, and they like warm weather."

"That's ridiculous, Odo Whitley, mushroom people can't exist in solid rock at those temperatures and pressures. And how would they wind up in the New York City subway system?"

"Maybe they're rock people inside the Earth, but when they reach the surface, they turn into mushroom people."

"Even if that were true, why would they eat people?

That's a curious evolutionary adaptation for creatures from the center of the Earth. It's all nonsense and you know it."

"Of course it is, but it's fun. What could possibly be better than a movie about giant mushroom people running around New York City trying to eat everyone?"

Sephie pulled the gleaming heart-shaped gold locket from her pocket, opening it.

"I forgot my glasses, and this inscription is so small. Could you please read it out loud to me, Odo Whitley?"

If you enjoyed reading
The Translucent Boy and the
Girl Who Dreamed She Could Fly
please leave a short review or rating
on Amazon.com
Reviews are the lifeblood of indie publishers –
we can't survive without them!

If you have any comments or suggestions
or would like to be notified of upcoming book
releases and Free Kindle book day promotions,
please email me at
OrvilleMouse@gmail.com

Follow me at:
www.facebook.com/TomHoffmanAuthor/

Best wishes until we meet again,

Tom Hoffman

ABOUT THE AUTHOR

Tom Hoffman received a B.S. in psychology
from Georgetown University in 1972
and a B.A. in 1980 from the now-defunct
Oregon College of Art. He has lived in Alaska
with his wife since 1973. They have two
adult children and three adorable
grandchildren. Tom was a graphic designer
and artist for over 35 years.
Redirecting his imagination from art to
writing, he wrote his first novel,
The Eleventh Ring, at age 63.